CHILLING CHRISTMAS · TALES ·

CHILLING CHRISTMAS TALES

Horror stories for the festive season

Includes stories by
Joan Aiken · Gillian Cross · Robert Swindells

■SCHOLASTIC

Scholastic Children's Books,
Scholastic Publications Ltd.,
7-9 Pratt Street, London NW1 0AE. UK

Scholastic Inc.,
730 Broadway, New York, NY 10003, USA

Scholastic Canada Ltd.,
123 Newkirk Road, Richmond Hill,
Ontario, Canada L4C 3G5

Ashton Scholastic Pty Ltd.,
PO Box 579, Gosford, New South Wales,
Australia

Ashton Scholastic Ltd.,
Private Bag 1, Penrose, Auckland,
New Zealand

First published in hardback by Scholastic Publications Ltd, 1992
This edition published, 1993

This collection copyright © Scholastic Publications Ltd, 1992
Illustrations copyright © David Wyatt, 1992

ISBN 0 590 55333 X

Typeset by Goodfellow & Egan Phototypesetting, Cambridge
Made and printed by Richard Clay, Bungay, Suffolk

10 9 8 7 6 5 4 3 2 1

ACKNOWLEDGMENTS

All of the stories are original and appear for the first time in this volume.

The following are the copyright owners of the stories:

The Road from Rushout Wood © Joan Aiken, 1992
Christmas Past © David Belbin, 1992
I'll Be Seeing You © Jill Bennett, 1992
Snapdragon © Gillian Cross, 1992
The Megowl © Garry Kilworth, 1992
Unseelie Court © Tessa Krailing, 1992
The Old Corpse Road © K.M. Peyton, 1992
The Familiar © Susan Price, 1992
The Highwayman's Last Ride © Malcolm Rose, 1992
In the Bleak Midwinter © Robert Swindells, 1992

The publisher wishes to thank all of the above, and David Wyatt, the illustrator, for their work and enthusiasm for this collection.

ontents

SNAPDRAGON

Gillian Cross

 he tiny lights sparkled, reflected in all directions, as Tod and Ben slouched round the corner. Ben saw them twinkle like stars, through the tall, feathery leaves of the pot plant that Tod had just bought for his mother. Red and yellow and green stars. Bright pinpoints, scattered from top to bottom of the Christmas tree in the big bay window.

Three children crowded round the tree, staring at the lights and pointing at the little parcels hidden among the branches. Their mother reached over their heads to drape on the last strands of tinsel, and their father stood on a ladder, holding the star that was going on the very top.

The perfect Christmas Eve picture.

"*Ah*!" said Tod, sarcastically. "How *sweet*! Just hold this a moment, will you?"

Carelessly, he pushed the pot plant into Ben's hands, not even noticing that he was bending one of the leaves. His eyes were fixed on the bright Christmas window, and there was an angry flare to his nostrils.

Ben knew that look. It always meant trouble. But he couldn't escape, because he had taken the plant from Tod. "I don't think— " he began.

Tod ignored him. "Get behind the hedge. And keep your mouth shut."

Ben ducked down on the other side of the hedge and watched through a gap as Tod crept towards the door and reached for the bellpush.

DRRRRRRRRRRR!

An electric bell rang inside the house and Tod shot out of the garden and flung himself down beside Ben. His eyes were glittering and he was breathing fast as he watched the picture in the window splinter. The children turned away from the tree, and their mother disappeared.

A second later she flung open the door, with a smile that dissolved when she saw no one there. She looked briefly up and down the road, tossed her head and slammed the door. When she walked back into the sitting room, she pulled the curtains briskly.

"Stupid cow!" Tod said, with satisfaction. "Come on."

He sauntered away up the road, leaving Ben to trail behind with the plant. The broken leaf had snapped off, and Ben looked down to flick it on to the pavement. When he looked up, he saw that Tod had stopped again.

He was staring up at a first floor window. In the dim light of a bedside lamp, a little boy sat up in his bunk, watching his father fix a stocking to the end of the bed. He was chewing his teddy's ear, and his eyes were open very wide.

"Getting ready for Santa!" Tod spat into the gutter as Ben came up beside him. "Let's give them a bit of excitement while they're waiting."

He was at the front door while Ben was still thinking where to hide. Jamming his finger defiantly on the bellpush, he grinned over his shoulder as Ben scrambled into the shelter of the wall next door. Then, when the door began to open, he took two steps sideways, into the shadow of a big holly bush.

The little boy's father opened the door and his face twisted.

"Louts!" he yelled, into the dark garden. "Haven't you got anything better to do?"

Behind him, Ben saw the little boy drag his teddy to the top of the stairs.

"Daddy!" he whined. "You said we were going to do my stocking— "

The door shut, sharply, and Tod strolled out of his hiding place, looking pleased with himself.

"Where shall we go now?"

Ben shifted the plant pot to his other arm, catching it on the wall by mistake. "I can't hang around, Tod. Honest. I've got to get home. With it being Christmas Eve."

Tod's grin hardened. "Got to get back to your mummy? Your darling daddy will be worrying, will he? Go on then. Don't let me stop you." He wrenched the plant roughly out of Ben's hands.

"You don't have to— " Ben said, uneasily. "I mean, why don't you come too? Mum won't mind."

Tod didn't say anything. Just stood there, looking, waiting for Ben to crack.

Ben put his hands into his pockets, hesitating. "What time does your mum get in, then?"

"How should I know? Midnight? One o'clock? She's not going to stay stuck in on her own, with me, is she? With it being Christmas Eve."

Tod started to walk off up the road, elaborately slowly, not bothering to look back at Ben, who was trailing a foot or two behind.

"OK," Ben said, crossly. "I'll hang around for a bit. If you like. What are we going to do?"

"Dunno." Tod looked up and down the road. "How about— " Suddenly, he grinned. "Hey, let's knock the grey house."

He pointed ahead, at the big corner house that sprawled ahead of them. Its front was dark and hidden, shrouded by the overgrown bushes in the garden. But the low side fence let them see the bare wall that stretched back from the pavement.

"That's dumb. No one lives there. Only— " Ben's eyes flickered away from it.

"Only *ghosts?*" Tod looked tauntingly at him. "Oh, come *on*, Benno. We're not little kids any more. Anyway, what d'you call that?"

He pointed to the small window at the back of the side wall. Its curtains were half open and faintly, in the gap between them, Ben glimpsed a flickering blue light.

"How should I know what it is?"

"Gho-o-osts!" Tod said again, opening his eyes wide.

"Do us a favour!" Ben was trying to sound tough, but his voice snagged in his throat, and Tod whooped with triumph.

"They're watching telly, saphead! Come on."

Grabbing Ben's hand, he dragged him along the pavement to the front gate. The path to the house was long and dark, almost closed in by the overgrown bushes. Ben could hardly make out the front door at the far end.

"Scared?" Tod said, needling him.

"Oh yes! Sure!" said Ben.

But he couldn't get the right, sarcastic note in his voice and Tod was grinning as he unlatched the gate. "After you, ghostbuster."

Ben took a step into the garden. There was barely room to walk between the bushes. Their twigs caught at his clothes, and the leafless branches rustled dryly. Under his feet, the tiled path was slippery with old, wet moss.

But he couldn't back out. Tod was right behind him, so close that the tattered leaves of the pot plant were brushing his neck. Uneasily, he began to walk forwards, placing his feet very carefully so that he would not fall. He tried not to notice how the bushes closed him in, shutting out everything beyond the path except for the solid, dark shape of the front door.

They were there too soon. Ben stopped dead when he reached the stone steps that led up to the door. Leaning forwards, Tod whispered in his ear.

"Go on, then. Ring it."

"Me?" Ben swallowed.

"It's your turn, Benny-boy. I don't want to hog all the fun."

Tod's face was hidden in the shadows, but Ben could *hear* the taunting smile on it. Slowly he ran a finger over the cracked, splintering paint, and a flake broke off and caught under his fingernail. Then he reached up, and tugged at the bell-pull.

The silence exploded into a loud jangle of brass, just on the other side of the door. Ben snatched his hand away, but that didn't stop the noise. The bell was swinging wildly, and the noise went on. And on and on and on.

Pushing past Tod, Ben turned and ran for the gate. His breath caught in his throat and by the time he reached the pavement he was sweating. He didn't realise that Tod was not following until he heard his voice, swearing softly from the shadows.

"That's right! Save your own skin. What about me? Just going to leave me here to rot, are you?"

Ben put his head back into the tunnel of bushes. "Stop fooling about! Get out of there!"

"Yes *sir!* Just wait while I leap to my feet— "

The words were cut off short as Tod caught his breath. Even from the other end of the tunnel, Ben heard it quite plainly. He pushed the gate open and stepped back into the garden.

"If you're trying to trick me— "

"Think I'm daft?" Tod said bitterly. "I tripped over the bootscraper. Think I've broken my— "

15

He caught his breath again, and Ben crept back up the path, watching the front door all the time. Tod was slumped on the steps, with his head against the door frame. Ben grabbed his shoulders and tried to drag him to his feet, but Tod lashed out sideways with the pot, knocking Ben's hands away.

"Don't do that!"

"But you've got to get up. How are you going to walk?"

"I can't walk!" Tod snapped. "Unless you want me to be sick all over your shoes. You try knocking your ankle to bits."

Ben looked down helplessly. "Well – how about crawling?"

"Oh, wonderful! All the way home?"

Ben could imagine his sour, scornful expression. "What are you going to do, then?"

Tod wriggled round and grabbed at Ben's anorak. "*I'm* not going to do anything except go on lying here. But *you're* going to ring that bell again. And ask if they'll let you phone your darling daddy. I'll never get home unless someone brings a car for me."

"But no one came the last time I rang." Ben looked nervously at the bell-pull. "Maybe they won't— "

Tod's fingers twisted the corner of the anorak into a rope. "*Make* them come. We know there's someone there, because we saw the television light."

"But— "

"Go *on!*"

Ben grabbed the big brass knocker in the centre of the door, meaning to hammer as hard as he could. But as soon as he touched it, the door swung away from him, into the house. He was looking down a dark, narrow hall, with closed doors on either side.

"H-hallo?" he stammered. "Is there anyone there?"

No one answered, but he caught a glimpse of something like movement at the far end of the hall. The last door on the left was not quite shut, and cold blue light flickered in the opening. Raising his voice, Ben called again.

"Hallo?"

From behind the open door came a faint, cracked voice. "Down here."

Ben looked sideways at Tod, waiting for some clue about what to do. But it was still too dark to see his face. And anyway, he could guess what Tod would say.

He walked up the two stone steps and into the hall. Chill, damp air closed round him, lying against his cheeks and seeping up his nose. It seemed heavier than any air he had ever breathed before. He stopped for a second.

"What's the matter with you?" Tod dragged himself upright, clinging to the door frame with one hand and swinging the pot plant in the other. He hauled himself up the steps and then lurched sideways, to fling an arm round

Ben's neck. "Get a move on! I'll come with you – if you're *scared*."

Ben wanted to push him away, to insist on going on his own. But the cold air choked back the words and he let Tod's arm stay where it was. Slowly, without speaking, the two of them began to move down the hall.

The floor was made of stone tiles, and Tod's foot slapped down heavily each time he hopped, but no one came out to see what the noise was. Step by step, pausing every now and then for Tod to catch his breath, they drew nearer to the half-open door.

When they reached it, Tod transferred his weight to the wall and waved his free hand. "After you, sir."

"Hallo?" Ben said for the third time. He cleared his throat noisily and looked at the light that danced against the wall in front of him. *Television*, Tod had said. But it wasn't. It was too blue for that.

On the other side of the door, there was a faint sound, like feet moving on a carpet. "Come in," said the cracked, old voice.

Ben pushed at the door and it swung away from him. For a second, he glimpsed the dark shapes of scattered chairs. Then the door opened wider, and he couldn't look at anything except the long table in the middle of the room.

And the fire.

There was a wide, shallow dish in the centre of the table, and it was full of blue fire, burning in a shallow, luminous layer. The flames wriggled and flickered from side to side, like live creatures, constantly moving, and the shadows of the room moved with them, swaying and twisting grotesquely.

The figure crouched over the fire was moving as well. She stood with her back to them, stooped forward so that her ragged hair swung round her face. And her small, stiff body jerked, like the body of a bird. Forward. Back. Forward again. Her hand snatched at the fire, sharp and quick as a pecking beak.

"Please— " Ben said uncertainly.

She stopped, with her hand halfway to the fire, but she didn't turn. Only her head tilted slightly, waiting for what was coming.

"We need to use your phone," Tod said. "I can't— "

"No phone!"

Suddenly, startlingly, she laughed, snatching at the fire again and then whirling round, with her hands stretched out towards them.

Fire danced on her fingertips.

They burned blue, licked by little flames that snaked towards the first joint and then shrank back again. The light distorted her smile, making her nose sharp and bright-pointed, and plunging her eyes into deep shadow.

19

Tod grabbed at Ben's shoulder. "What the— "

The old woman waved her hands at them and laughed again, baring her teeth. The blue light danced on stained fangs, scattered survivors in a mouthful of empty spaces.

"Coming to play?" she hissed. "Or are you scared?"

"Can't see anything to be scared of."

Tod said it defiantly, but his voice was too loud and the laugh came again, like the wind in dead leaves. "Come and play Snapdragon!"

She beckoned them slowly, with a shrunken hand that suddenly darted away, into the centre of the fire. Ben saw her snatch up something and cram it into her mouth.

"Let's get out of here," he muttered.

"Are you crazy?" Tod was staring at the blue fire. His tongue flicked quickly over his top lip. "I'm going to play."

He grabbed at Ben's shoulder and forced him forward, hopping just behind. Together, they lurched towards the table, Tod's foot thudding on the thin carpet. As soon as they were near enough, he seized a chair and flopped down into it, dumping the remains of his mother's plant on the table.

"Now!" he said. His tongue flicked again, catching the corner of his mouth, and Ben heard him breathing, shallow and fast.

"Tod!" he hissed. "Don't— "

But Tod's hand was already hovering over the fire, wavering uncertainly as he peered into it.

The old woman tipped her head sideways, her mouth twisting into a mocking smile – and Tod grabbed.

His hand came out flaming blue at the fingertips, and Ben gasped, before he could stop himself.

"Tod— "

"Don't be soft!" Tod snapped. "It doesn't hurt." He pushed something into his mouth and grinned up at the old woman. "Almonds!"

She laughed her thin, rustling laugh. "Sweet or bitter?"

"They're good." Tod nudged Ben. "Come on. Try it." He dipped into the tray again, feeling round greedily, and then snatched his hand away and swore.

The old woman tittered in the shadows. "Be *quick!*" Her hand darted in and out, and Ben heard the almond crunch between her ruined teeth.

The flames were beginning to die, dwindling and shrinking in towards the middle of the tray. As they grew smaller, Ben stretched his hand out, trying to pluck up courage to plunge in.

"Do it like this!" Tod snatched again, laughing as he waved a flaming raisin under Ben's nose.

"Like this!" The old woman grabbed a fistful of almonds and tipped them in a burning stream from one hand to the other.

"Before it's too late!" Tod pushed Ben's hand down towards

the last patch of blue, but Ben pulled it back automatically, shrinking away from the fire.

And then he'd missed it.

The last little flames ran along one side of the tray and dwindled into tiny, formless blobs. Then they went out, and the room was dark.

The old woman gave a long sigh. "Turn on the light."

"The— ?" Ben looked stupidly at the tray, and she stamped her foot.

"By the door!"

Picking his way across the room, Ben fumbled round the door frame and flicked the switch. He didn't realise how frightened he had been until the shadows dissolved – and left him standing in an ordinary, shabby dining room. The flat brightness of electric light lit up worn chairs and stained wallpaper, without any sign of Christmas to brighten the drabness. No tinsel, no decorations, not even a Christmas card.

The only unusual thing was the old tin tray on the table. Nuts and raisins were scattered all over it and round them was a trickle of dark brown liquid.

Tod dipped a finger into it and tasted it. "Brandy?"

The old woman chuckled. "I had half a bottle in there."

The words sounded comfortable and ordinary and, in the light, she was ordinary too. Small and shrivelled, with a bony nose and liver-spotted hands. The only strange thing about her was the blue bow in her straggling white hair.

Ben was so relieved that he almost laughed. *"Brandy?"*

"Of course," she said gravely. "We always had a snapdragon on Christmas Eve. Everyone played it in those days, and we were crazy about it. Mother had to fight to save enough brandy for the pudding. The boys always tried to wheedle some more. *Give us another go, Ma! The pudding won't need all that!* She got so cross with them!" The dry old voice creaked into laughter and she stroked the rim of the tray with one finger.

Just an old-fashioned Christmas game! Ben turned to grin at Tod, to share the joke.

But Tod wasn't watching him. He was staring admiringly at the old woman. "I bet it wasn't just the boys she got cross with. I bet you nagged her worse than they did. You're so good at it. Much better than I am."

She flicked the rim of the tray, so that it rang like a bell. And when she spoke again, her voice was cold. "Oh, they never let me play. I was too young." For a moment she looked sulky, like a bad-tempered child.

"Make up for it now, then." Tod put his elbows on the table. "Let's have another game."

"I really ought to go— " Ben said, reluctantly, but Tod snorted.

"Don't be so *wet*. You haven't even tried it yet. I think we ought to have another game."

"You do?" The old woman looked steadily at Tod for a moment, and Ben suddenly noticed how blue her eyes were. A clear, startling blue, as bright as her ribbon.

"Why not?" Tod said. "Have you got any more brandy?"

"It's in the kitchen." The blue eyes suddenly swivelled round to Ben. "You can go and get it if you like. Across the hall."

Ben shuffled his feet. "Really – my mum and dad are expecting me – I promised— "

"Such a *good* little boy!" Tod rolled his eyes up at the ceiling. "Why don't you set the snapdragon burning first? Then you can leave me here while you go and get your dad."

The old woman smiled at Ben, tilting her head on one side. "You can use all the rest of the brandy. Put it in the saucepan to warm— "

"I know how to do it," muttered Ben. "I've watched Dad, when he does it for the pudding."

"Aren't you the lucky one," Tod said sourly. "With a darling daddy who's around at Christmas. And a precious mummy who bothers with Christmas puddings." He flicked the tin tray with his fingernail, as the old woman had done, and then dropped his head, listening as it rang.

Ben walked across the hall, found the kitchen and

switched on the light. There was grease on the rickety old table and the sink was cracked, but he saw the brandy bottle straight away. It stood by the cooker, with a small saucepan and a box of matches next to it. Unscrewing the top, he poured all the brandy into the saucepan.

The gas seemed to take a long time to come through, and the first match burnt right down to his fingers. But at last the flame came, with a vigorous pop, and he stood the saucepan over it. As the brandy began to warm, he caught the familiar, mixed, once-a-year smells of brandy and gas and burnt matches.

And he wanted to be at home.

His mother would be in the kitchen, swigging sherry and making mince pies. And Dad would be teasing Mary and Laura, pretending that he couldn't find the stockings. What was he doing in this cold, dark house, with no one but Tod and a stranger?

Lighting another match, Ben held it over the saucepan until the brandy caught fire with a small, soft explosion. Then he walked across the hall, calling as he went.

"Coming! Are you ready?"

The old woman flicked the light off as he went into the dining room and he carried the panful of blue flames over to the table.

"Here we go, then. Happy Christmas!"

He poured out the brandy in a steady, glowing stream, until the tray was a sea of fire again. Then he swung the saucepan away.

"OK. I'm off."

But he hesitated for a second, waiting to be persuaded out of it. Waiting for Tod to say, *Stay a bit* or *Have a turn before you go*.

Only Tod wasn't thinking about him at all. He just flapped a vague hand in Ben's direction and muttered, "Great. See you in a minute." His eyes were on the flames, and his hand was already hovering over the tray, ready to pounce.

But the old woman beat him to it. Her hand dived forward, into the very centre of the flames.

"A raisin!"

"Don't pinch them all! " Tod grabbed too, and grinned at her as he pushed two almonds into his mouth.

For a second, Ben watched them. Then he walked out of the room and down the dark hall. As he pulled the front door shut behind him, he could see the orange brightness of street lights at the other end of the tunnel of bushes, and he heard the church clock strike seven. Mary and Laura's bedtime.

He started to run, but he didn't get far Halfway up the hill, a car slid along the pavement and drew up beside him, and his father leaned over to open the passenger door.

"Where have you been? The girls are ready to hang up their stockings, and you promised you'd be back to do yours at the same time."

"I was just coming. But Tod— "

"Groan!" His father pulled a face. "Couldn't he spare you for once? It *is* Christmas."

"He's hurt his ankle," Ben said. "Maybe even broken it." He slid into the car and pulled the door shut. "We'll have to give him a lift home, Dad."

His father gave another dramatic groan. "No use taking him home. I don't suppose that mother of his will be around to look after him. We'd better get him straight to Casualty. Where is he?"

"In the grey house." Ben pointed.

His father looked sharply at him. "Have you been breaking in?"

"Of course not! The old lady asked us to go in."

"Old lady?"

"She's living there now."

There was another sharp look, but his father didn't say anything. He just turned left at the bottom of the hill and pulled up outside the grey house.

Ben was out of the car while the engine was still running. "I'll get him."

The path between the bushes was still dark, but this time

his father was watching from beyond the gate. Ben strode up to the door and tugged hard at the bell-pull.

He knew he would have to wait. Tod couldn't get to the door and it would take the old woman some time to walk down the hall. Ben stood with his arms folded, listening for the sound of feet.

But no one came.

The car door slammed, and his father walked up the path. "Having problems?"

"No one's answering." Ben frowned. "They *must* be able to hear— "

His father was examining the door, tapping at the top and the bottom of it. "This feels as though it's boarded up on the inside."

"But that's impossible! We went in— " Ben swallowed, and stopped.

"I'm going round the back," his father said, abruptly. "I'll see if I can get in that way."

He dived off to the right, pushing his way through the bushes, and Ben stood looking after him for a moment. Then he remembered the side window. He struggled the other way through the bushes and ran down the side path.

He could see the little window ahead of him, with its curtains still half open and the gap lit by that blue glow that Tod had mistaken for the light from a television. Heading straight for it, he ploughed across a flower bed and pressed his nose to the glass.

And there they were. Two figures, facing each other across the blazing snapdragon. Tod was grinning and laughing out loud as his hands dipped into the tray and came out flaming bright. He tossed the nuts and raisins into the air, catching them between his teeth and gazing tauntingly over the table as he chewed them with his mouth open.

The person on the other side of the table laughed back at him, her perfect white teeth gleaming in the blue light. She had pushed her brown curls back over her shoulder and they bounced on the lacy collar of her velvet dress as she bobbed forward towards the tray.

Beyond, the feathery plant spread its leaves like a tiny, moonlit tree, every delicate, beautiful frond dancing as the flames danced. Light winked back from gleaming, polished wood and bright festoons of tinsel. Glasses twinkled on a sideboard where bottles stood shoulder to shoulder, and a plateful of mince pies lay next to a big, iced cake. Every inch of the room was warm and glittering and full of Christmas.

For a second, Ben was hollow with longing to be there, to be part of that perfect Christmas Eve picture. But he knew it was too late. He couldn't get back now.

Raising his hand, he knocked on the window.

The girl whirled round to face him, and he had one

glimpse of her unmistakable blue eyes. Blue as the ribbon that tied up her curls. Then the last flame on the tray flickered and shrank to nothing, and the snapdragon went out.

At the same moment, there was a sound of splintering wood as the back door gave way. Then heavy footsteps echoed from the tiled hall and his father called out to him.

"It's like I said, Ben. There's nobody here. Nobody at all."

IN THE BLEAK MIDWINTER

Robert Swindells

I don't see why we always have to spend Christmas at Grandma's," said Kevin, handing his father the overnight bag he'd just packed. "I mean, it's so boring. Why can't we have an exciting Christmas for once, like Heather and her family – they're off skiing in Austria."

"Yes," agreed Sally. "Or why aren't we back-packing to Katmandu like the Stanleys? It's one big yawn at Grandma's, Dad. It's always the same. Church on Christmas Eve. Pressies round the tree Christmas morning, a gigantic dinner at lunchtime followed by a walk that's meant to sharpen our appetites for an enormous tea nobody wants. Yawn, Yawn."

It was the afternoon of Christmas Eve and the Teals were about to set off in the family car for Fawley, some seventy miles away. When they were small, Kevin and Sally had loved their Christmas at Grandma's, but now Kevin was fifteen and Sally fourteen and they'd grown out of it. It was no use protesting, though – they both knew that. Grandma's for Christmas had become a family tradition and Grandma's it would be, no matter what.

At three o'clock, Dad finished packing the car and said, "Righto, folks – two minutes to liftoff. Pulled all the plugs out, Mother?" He said exactly the same thing every year, always at three o'clock. Kevin caught his sister's eye and they swapped grimaces. "I hereby declare the twelfth Great Annual Bore open," he murmured.

It was cold outside, with a sky full of low, sullen cloud. Dad switched the heater on and by the time they'd driven a mile it was like a sauna inside the car. Kevin pulled out the neck of his sweater and blew down it.

"Don't do that with your sweater!" rapped Mum. "You'll have it all out of shape."

"Doesn't matter," said Kevin gloomily. "Grandma'll have knitted me a new one for Christmas. She always does."

They'd been on the road twenty minutes when it began to snow. It was nothing much at that stage – a mere sprinkling of fine flakes, but Sally eyed it hopefully.

"Hey, Dad!" she said, "Maybe we'd better turn back. There's that stretch across the moors, you know. It can get very bad up there."

"Rubbish!" Dad's tone was scornful. "It's a twelve-mile stretch and we'll reach it in another twenty minutes. Even if it goes on snowing we'll be across before there's an inch."

"And anyway," put in Mum, "it won't go on snowing. There've only been two white Christmases in my lifetime."

They drove on in silence, Kevin and Sally gazing glumly out at the passing scene, dreaming of ski slopes and Katmandu. The snowfall thickened. The flakes were larger now and there were more of them. Dad muttered something and switched on the wipers. Mum, who had had her window down an inch, wound it up.

"Dad," began Sally, but her father growled that he was concentrating, and so she said no more.

A wind had arisen, blowing from their right. It drove the snowflakes diagonally across the road ahead, which was becoming covered. They were going uphill now, up onto the moors, and once there came a shrill squeal as the tyres failed to grip, and spun. Mum shot a questioning glance at Dad, who ignored it. In the back, Kevin and Sally exchanged looks. He was okay, Dad, but there was a stubbornness in him which could make him determined to do whatever he was advised not to do. They were becoming worried, but they offered no advice.

When they reached the high ground the scale of their problem grew plain. The road was covered to a depth of at least four inches, and in those places where it was most exposed the crosswind was laying drifts from verge to verge. So far these were no more than a foot or so high, but the way the stuff was coming down made it obvious that the road would soon be impassable.

Sally watched the back of her father's head. He'd give up now, surely? Turn the car around and head back to low ground while there was still a chance of reaching home. Mum was watching him too, and Sally knew she was wondering whether to say something. In the event, it was Kevin who spoke.

"Dad," he said, "this is stupid. Everybody else has turned back." It was true, but it was the worst thing he could have said.

"Stupid?" The back of Dad's neck glowed red. "Are you saying I'm stupid, son?"

"N – no, Dad. At least – yes, maybe I am in this particular case. I mean, we don't have to go on, do we? It's not absolutely crucial, is it?"

"It's a promise, son. A commitment. I told your grandma we'd be there and we will."

"But she'll see the weather report. She won't expect—."

"Drop it, son. I gave my word and that's it. I know you never wanted to come, but my word's my bond and it'll take more than a few flakes of snow to make me break it."

Kevin threw up his hands in exasperation but said no more. Let him go on then, he thought. Let him get us all stuck on this stupid moor for a week, then maybe he'll be satisfied.

They ploughed on. The wind was now gusting strongly enough to send shudders through the car, and it drove the snow so thickly across the road that visibility was practically zero. Sally had been keeping an eye on the mileometer. There'd been eighty-six thousand, four hundred and twenty-one miles on the clock when they'd reached the high ground, and the digits had rolled over with agonising slowness since then. "Twelve miles," urged a voice inside her head. "Carry us twelve more miles, please." But when the vehicle slewed and stopped they'd done just five.

"Shovel!" rapped Dad, before anyone could speak. "Kevin, get the shovel from the boot and dig through that drift. Mother, Sally, pile out and get set to push when I say. It's only a bit of a drift – we'll be on our way in no time."

They weren't. The shrieking wind rebuilt the drift faster than Kevin could shovel, and pushing accomplished nothing except that mother and daughter were quickly soaked and frozen. They got back inside and slammed the doors.

Dad, dry and undaunted, spoke. "Right. Stay with your vehicle. That's what the experts advise. Run the engine to keep warm."

"And when the petrol runs out?" queried Sally, shivering.

"Shut up!" rapped Dad. "You're the one who wanted an exciting Christmas."

"So we wait," said Mum, looking sidelong at her husband. "What exactly do we wait *for*, dear?"

"Rescue, of course," Dad snapped. "Your mother knows we're coming. When we don't arrive she'll try phoning us, and when there's no reply she'll know we're somewhere en route. As Kevin pointed out, she'll have seen the weather report, so she'll alert the authorities. We'll be out of here in a jiffy."

Mum said nothing, though she longed to. If you hadn't been so idiotically pig-headed. Something like that, but it was pointless. It would probably provoke a row, poisoning an atmosphere which was quite bad enough already.

They sat, not speaking. The only sounds were the whine and slam of the wind, the ticking of snowflakes on the windows, the stuttering purr of the motor and the occasional shush of the wipers as Dad tried to keep the windscreen clear.

Sally peered through the window. She could no longer see where the verge began. The road had disappeared and it was almost dark.

"What's the time?" she asked, to break the silence.

"Thirteen minutes past four," Mum told her. "Why?"

"I just wondered."

"How long do we give it?" queried Kevin.

"What d'you mean, how long do we give it?" Dad sounded irritated.

"Before we get out and walk," said Kevin. "Do we wait till the petrol's gone or should one of us go and look for a farm or something before it's completely dark?"

"There are no farms for miles," Dad told him. "I remember from previous years. We sit tight, all of us, till help arrives. It won't be long now."

"I need a pee," murmured Sally.

"Oh, yes! Well, you would, wouldn't you?" Dad snapped. "Just when we've built up some nice heat in here. Why is it that wherever—."

"Dad," remonstrated Mum. "The child can't help it if she has to go." She turned. "Off you go, love. Close the door, but don't lose sight of the car."

Sally was back in a minute and a half, brushing snow from her shoulders. "Brr!" she shuddered. "It's absolutely dreadful out there, but I think I saw a light."

"A light?" said Dad sharply. "Where?"

Sally leaned forward and pointed. "Somewhere over there, I think. It wasn't very bright – just a sort of glimmer, and I couldn't see it all the time."

"Imagination." Dad peered through the windscreen. "I don't see anything."

"I do!" cried Mum. "Or at least I did, just for a second. There!" She pointed.

"Oh, yes." Dad nodded. "Spotted it myself that time. Right." He undid his seat belt.

"What are you going to do?" asked Mum.

"I thought I might take all my clothes off and roll about in the snow for a bit," replied Dad sarcastically. "What d'you think I'm going to do? You wait here."

The wind had piled snow against the car's offside and he had to shove quite hard to get his door open. He turned, yelling against the wind.

"Switch on the headlights so I can find my way back." An Arctic blast filled the car with swirling flakes before the door slammed and he was gone.

"Silly old fart!" snarled Kevin.

"That'll do," said Mum. "Your dad's doing his best. There's no need for language."

"If he hadn't—" began Sally.

"I know, I know. He's a stubborn man and he's landed us in this ridiculous mess but he realises that, and going on about it won't solve anything. We must all do what we can to get out of it – that's all."

* * *

It was seven minutes before Dad returned, caked from chin to knee in white. He'd lost his hat.

"It's a house," he gasped. "About four hundred yards away. Switch off the lights and the engine and follow me."

Kevin shoved open his door and scrambled out. As he straightened up the wind flayed his face so that he gasped and flung up his hands to shield his eyes. The snow was knee-high and he could feel it filling his light shoes. Mum and Sally were trudging with their heads down, following Dad's blurred form into the teeth of the blizzard. Kevin felt those teeth as he lurched after them.

As they approached the house, the Teals saw that the light which had drawn them was escaping through the thin curtain of a window beside the door. The door itself was enclosed in a small stone porch and into this they stumbled, thankful for the protection it afforded against the wind. As they stood in a fog of breath, stamping snow from their ruined footwear, a dog began to bark inside.

Dad knocked with purple knuckles on the solid looking door. For a while nothing happened except that the barking grew more frenzied.

"Don't like the sound of that," said Mum.

"Lonely spot," Dad replied. "I'd want a good dog if I lived here."

He was about to knock again when they heard a voice,

39

apparently cursing the dog. The barking stopped. A door slammed, and shuffling footsteps approached. A bolt was drawn and a crack of light appeared as the door opened slightly.

"Who's there?" the same voice demanded. "What do you want?"

Dad squinted into the narrow opening. There was a stout chain, and beyond it a slice of grizzled face.

"There are four of us," he said. "A family. Our car's stuck in a snowdrift. Could we possibly come in – use your phone or something?"

"No phone," the voice replied. "Don't believe in 'em. You can come in though, of course."

The slice of face disappeared as the speaker closed the door and removed the chain. When it opened, a little wider this time, it revealed a very tall, very thin man of about sixty, wearing a baggy fawn cardigan, crumpled corduroy trousers and trodden-down carpet slippers bound to his feet with elastic bands. His head was long and narrow, and bald except for the silver stubble on his cheeks and a semicircle of long, fine hair which looked as though it could do with a wash.

The man smiled, revealing three or four long, crooked teeth which reminded Kevin for some reason of a beaver.

"Well," he crooned. "You have landed yourselves in a

mess, haven't you? Leave your shoes and come through." He stepped back and the four Teals entered, noticing a faint, unpleasant smell as they did so.

They were standing in a dimly-lit hallway with a staircase and three doorways. Behind one door they could hear the dog, whining and scratching at the woodwork. The man noticed Mum's nervous glance.

"Pay no heed to old Rags, Missus," he said. "He don't take kindly to callers but he's harmless when he gets to know you."

Mum didn't find this particularly reassuring, especially when the animal began hurling itself at the door, but she smiled and nodded. They discarded their sodden shoes and followed the man along the hallway and through a doorway into the room through whose curtain they had seen the light.

It was a shabby, cluttered room with a threadbare carpet over which lay strewn newspapers and items of clothing. A three-piece suite sagged shapelessly before the meagre fire which flickered on a hearth whose cracked and grubby tiles supported a plate and a couple of unwashed mugs. As they entered, the man took their dripping coats and draped them over chairs in various parts of the room, assuring them that they'd dry out in no time.

"Sit down," he invited, indicating the suite. "Make yourselves comfy." He smiled. "You'll have to excuse the mess – not used to company, me and Rags. Hot drink?"

"Oooh, yes please," said Mum, holding out her hands to the flames while the others made appreciative noises. The old fellow's house was obviously none too clean and none of them was really keen to sup in it, but there was nothing wrong with their manners and they were guests, weren't they?

Their host shuffled away. Kevin rubbed his hands together.

"Bit chilly in here, isn't it?"

"Ssh!" Mum pressed a finger to her lips. "He might hear. And anyway it's warmer than out there." She nodded towards the chimney in which the wind boomed and racketed.

"Certainly is," agreed Dad. "Good job I spotted the place, eh?" His family exchanged covert glances but refrained from comment.

"I wonder if he'll let us stay the night?" said Sally. "Can't say I fancy it."

"Of course he will," Dad told her. "There's no alternative, unless the rescue services reach the car tonight, which doesn't seem likely."

"You said they'd be here any moment," protested Kevin.

"No I didn't. And anyway, conditions have changed since then. It's snowing far more heavily now."

The old man returned with four steaming mugs on a tin tray, which he set down on the sticky looking hearthrug.

"There y'are – that'll drive out the chill."

"What is it?" asked Kevin. His mother shot him a scowl.

42

"Cocoa," their host replied. "Finest thing there is in rough weather." He winked at Kevin. "Twelve years in the Navy taught me that."

"Were you in the War?" asked Sally politely.

"Aye, that I was. Three years, Malta to Murmansk, till I stopped a bit of metal with my noggin. Look." He lifted the hair from the right side of his face, revealing a livid indentation which ran from the temple to somewhere behind the ear, the tip of which was missing. Sally winced.

"It's a wonder you weren't killed."

"Aye, lass, it is, and it was nip and tuck for a spell too, but I'm none the worse now, thank the Lord, whatever some folk say."

Sally wanted to ask what it was that folk said, but she didn't. She sipped her cocoa and smiled with her eyes at the old man through the steam.

"I suppose you can put us up till morning?" asked Dad. The fellow nodded.

"No trouble. Berths for all up above. You'll not get away for a day or two, I reckon."

"Oh, but we couldn't possibly impose on your hospitality for so long." Mum looked dismayed. Their host cackled, showing his crooked teeth.

"Snow'll be six foot deep by morning, Missus. Yon road's blocked three days many a time."

Mum looked at Dad.

"Grandma will be dreadfully worried and we can't even phone. I feel ever so guilty."

Dad shook his head.

"Don't feel guilty, love. Circumstances beyond our control and all that. She's a level-headed old lass – she'll know what to do."

They drank their cocoa while the wind roared around the house. When they'd finished, the old man collected their mugs and carried the tray away, returning a few moments later with the snarling, struggling dog, which he held by its collar.

"Now, Rags," he soothed, "these people are friends. Friends. They'll be staying, understand?"

Rags gave no sign that he understood, but when their host let him go he didn't tear out anybody's throat. Instead he went from one guest to another, sniffing their knees before settling himself with a final growl on the hearthrug.

"There y'are," the old man smiled. "All mates. He won't bother you now as long as you stay in the house."

Kevin thought this an odd remark. He wanted to ask what Rags would do if one of them went outside. Instead he said, "What sort is he?"

"Border Collie. Finest breed alive. Ever seen 'em working sheep?"

Kevin nodded. "On telly. It's unbelievable how intelligent they are."

"That's right, lad. Brighter than some people I've known, I can tell you."

"We know your dog's name," smiled Dad, "but not yours."

"Shaw," said their host at once. "Ben Shaw. And yours?"

"Teal," Dad told him. "David and Margaret, Kevin and Sally."

The old man nodded. "So, now we're properly introduced, what shall we do? There's a long evening ahead."

Sally felt like saying, "You could build the fire up for a start," but instead she said, "Tell us about the war – your adventures and that."

"Adventures?" Old Shaw cackled. "War's not adventures, lass. War's being bored and scared sick, both at the same time. It's sadness and madness and squalor and waste – that's what war is, but if you really want to hear about it I'll tell you. It'll pass the time."

They sat hugging themselves for warmth while the old man told of convoys to Malta and to Russia, of dive-bombers and torpedoes and seas so cold they'd freeze the life out of a man in less than a minute. He spoke about asdic and depth-charges and the tell-tale oil-slick which means you've killed a sub. He told them of mates who had died and others who had not, of shore leaves at Malta and Gibraltar, Archangel and Murmansk, till Sally wondered how it was that a man who had been to such faraway places and seen and done so much with such good friends could end up living like a hermit on the moors with only a dog for company. And when at last he'd told all his stories, she was surprised on glancing at her watch to find it was almost ten o'clock.

Mum also noticed the time. "Well," she said, stretching and yawning, "you've certainly led an eventful life, Mr Shaw. It's been fascinating listening to your stories, but now I think we'd better get some sleep if that's all right."

"Of course, Mrs Teal, but you'll take a spot of supper before you turn in?"

Mum would have declined, but Kevin said, "I will," and Dad said "Mmm – that'll be nice," so she smiled and nodded.

"I don't want anything," said Sally. "I'm not hungry, thanks."

Old Shaw went off, presumably to the kitchen. Kevin started to get up, intending to look out of the window, but when Rags opened one eye and growled he sank back in his chair.

"This is weird," whispered Sally. "I wish we weren't staying, Dad."

"Now don't be ungrateful, Sally," Dad reproved. "Mr Shaw's been very kind."

"What if someone arrives during the night," asked Kevin, "and finds the car? They won't know where we are."

"That's right," said Mum. "They'll think we've wandered off. Perhaps one of us ought to—" She'd been about to suggest that somebody sit up and keep an eye on the road, but the old man appeared at that moment with the supper tray.

He must have overheard because he said, "Don't you worry about that, Mrs Teal. What I'll do is, I'll leave the light on in here when I go to bed. Anybody on the road'll spot it, as you did yourselves. They'll know you're here because there's nowhere else for miles. How's that?"

"Well – yes, that's fine I suppose," Mum replied. "It's just that I wouldn't want people searching for us and us tucked up in bed."

Supper was sardine sandwiches and more cocoa. Shaw handed round mugs.

"Here, lass." He held one out to Sally. "I know you said you weren't hungry, but a nice drop of cocoa'll send you off like a babby."

"Thanks," smiled Sally, though in fact she was irritated.

She sat warming her hands on the mug while the others ate and drank. Sardines weren't what they'd have chosen for supper, but the cold had made them hungry and soon the plate held only one sandwich, which old Shaw gave to Rags.

"Right, then." He got to his feet. "Follow me and I'll show you the rooms."

They followed. Sally waited till the old man was through the doorway, then looked around for a way to dispose of her cocoa. She'd hoped there'd be a plant or something but there wasn't, so she shrugged and put the mug on the hearth. To her delight, Rags immediately roused himself and, thrusting his muzzle into it, began to lap noisily.

"Good, boy, Rags," she grinned, and hurried after the others.

The stairs creaked and the air was so cold they could see their breath. A dim bulb dangled over the stairwell so that it was not completely dark, but beyond the staircase the shadows thickened. Sally followed the others till the old man stopped to push open a door.

"This one's for the young 'uns. They won't mind sharing, I suppose?"

"No, no – not at all," Mum assured him. Shaw moved on to the next door. "And this is yours. Bathroom's at the end there, and I trust you'll be comfortable. G'night."

"Good night, Mr Shaw," Dad replied. "And thank you."

Sally was about to add her own good night when she became aware of a warm draught round her ankles. She was standing near a door, and the warmth seemed to be coming from under it. As the old man approached her on his way to the stairs she said, "What's this room, Mr Shaw? It's lovely and warm just here." She imagined Rags rounding up every scrap of warmth in the house and driving it through this doorway like penning sheep.

"That one?" Shaw seemed off-balance for a second, then he smiled. "Orchids, lass. Little hobby of mine. Tropical, see? Gotta keep 'em snug."

"Orchids!" cried Mum, approaching in her stockinged feet. "Oh, Mr Shaw, I love orchids. D'you think I might – just the tiniest peep?"

"Sorry." Their host stationed himself between her mother and the door with a haste Sally considered unnecessary. "Not tonight, Mrs Teal. Open this door tonight and they're goners, the lot of 'em. I'll show you in the morning when it's not so cold."

"Orchids," murmured Sally, as she joined Kevin in the room they were condemned to share. "Whoever would have thought it?"

"Hmmm," went Kevin.

"These beds!" Sally ran her palms over one. "Lumpy, damp and narrow, just as I expected."

"Hmmm," said her brother. Sally looked at him.

"Is that all you can say?"

"Hmm — I'm tired, Sal. Shattered. Gotta get some sleep." He was peeling off his jumper.

"I'd keep that on if I were you," Sally advised. "It's Arctic in here. I'm leaving everything on and I bet I still don't sleep."

She didn't. At least, not for some time. She lay with frozen feet while Kevin snored. There was a small, empty fireplace in which the wind boomed, dislodging clots of soot which fell rattling on the grate. It was almost completely dark, and the smell she'd noticed on entering the house was stronger here.

She must have dozed off in spite of everything because she woke with a start to find the room grown silent. The wind had dropped and the sky must have cleared because there was a square of pale moonlight on the floor. Kevin had stopped snoring, but something had woken her. She listened. For a while there was nothing, but then she became aware of a bumping, slithering noise which seemed to come from beyond the door. It was as though something heavy was being dragged along the landing. She imagined she could hear heavy breathing, but that might be Kevin. As she lay, damp with fear, the noise grew louder. The thing out there, whatever it was, was right outside the room now.

"Don't come in," she prayed, her eyes fixed on the door. "Please don't." There was a moment of silence during which she didn't dare breathe, and then the dragging noise resumed.

Swiftly she slipped out of bed and crossed the room.

"Kev!" She shook her brother. "Hey, Kev – something's going on." She pulled his sleeve and hissed into his ear but Kevin didn't stir.

Out on the landing the noise continued for a while, then stopped. Sally froze over her brother's bed, straining her ears. She heard a click, a creak, and then the dragging again, muffled now.

"Kev!" She punched his arm. "Wake up for pete's sake!"

Kevin grunted, turned over and began to snore.

"What the heck's up with you?" she sobbed. "It's like you're out on—" She gasped. Dope. Out on dope. She remembered the cocoa. They'd all drunk it except her. And what was that the old weirdo had said – it'll send you off like a babby? Could it be – was it possible that he'd put something in the cocoa? But why? Why should he? Was he a murderer or something?

Stuffing a fist in her mouth to keep from crying, Sally crossed to the window, lifted the thin curtain and looked down. The light had gone. When they'd been preparing for bed, she and Kevin had looked down and seen how the light from the downstairs window had cast a rectangle of yellow on the snow. Now there was nothing. Old Shaw had turned out the light. Broken his promise. Why?

Mum and Dad. She must go to Mum and Dad. She must open that door and slip along the landing. It wasn't far. Ten paces. Twelve at the most. Yes, but what if—? She sobbed, gnawing her knuckles. So many "what ifs". The cocoa. The slithering. Rags.

She turned back to the window and peered towards the invisible road. "Please, God," she prayed, "send someone – a snowplough, anything. I don't know what to do."

She did, though. She knew exactly what she was going to have to do, and the longer she delayed the worse it would be. With a final glance at her unconscious brother, she tiptoed to the door. She put her ear to the crack and listened. Nothing. With infinite care she felt for the doorknob, wrapped her hand round it and slowly, very slowly, twisted it. There was a click which sounded to Sally like a bomb going off, and the door inched open. When she had a four-inch gap she pressed her face to it and swivelled her eyes, trying to see both ways along the landing. She saw nothing but darkness. She took half a step backwards and eased the door fully open. It creaked faintly, but the sound brought no nightmare form roaring and reaching out of the blackness. Silently, holding the door frame and her breath, she stepped out onto the landing.

Left. Mum and Dad's room was next on the left, and if she remembered correctly there'd been nothing between – no chair or table she might fall over. So. If she let her left hand touch the wall all the way she couldn't possibly go wrong, blind as she was. She left the door open and moved off, thinking, where's Rags?

I wish I had my shoes, she thought. I feel horribly vulnerable in my socks, as though if something attacked me I wouldn't be able to defend myself effectively. No sooner had this thought crossed her mind than she felt a tense, creeping sensation at the back of her head and turned, peering with slitted eyes into the blackness. There was no sound, but her imagination conjured a sly shifting of black against black: the stealthy advance of a shadow in the shadows. She watched for a moment, half expecting to be seized, but the phantoms mocked her, weaving and bobbing just beyond reach. She dragged her gaze from them and went on till her trailing knuckles found the frame of her parents' door.

It was open. She could see this because the window spilled moonlight on the floor, and as she slipped thankfully into the room there was sufficient light to reveal two beds: one occupied, the other rumpled but empty. She crossed to the occupied bed.

"Mum! Wake up, Mum. Where's Dad?" Even as she shook her mother's shoulder a part of her knew it was useless. Her parents had drunk the cocoa too, which meant – which means I'm alone, she realised. Alone in this awful house with a crazy old man and a vicious dog. What the heck can I do? And where's Dad? He had cocoa. He can't possibly have woken up. Can he? Hope surged in her. She crossed the room, found the switch and snapped it on. A wedge of light illuminated the landing. She stood in the doorway, ready to slam the door if Rags appeared, and yelled "Dad? Dad, where are you?"

It'll bring old Shaw, she told herself. And the dog, but I don't care. Anything's better than creeping about in the dark, alone. "Daaad!"

As Sally's shout echoed through the house the door of the orchid room opened and the old man appeared, fully dressed and somewhat dishevelled. "What – how the devil—?"

"Where's my dad?" cried Sally. "What have you done to him?"

Then she was running – running towards old Shaw with bared teeth and flying hair. What she'd do when she reached him she didn't know, but instinct told her she must act now, before he recovered from the shock of finding her conscious, if she hoped to leave this house alive.

As the girl came at him, Shaw scrabbled at the orchid room door, cursing and gibbering as he tried to thrust a large key into its lock. He hadn't succeeded when Sally piled into him, fists flailing. Caught off balance by the ferocity of the attack he staggered sideways and toppled, crashing to the boards. The key flew from his grasp and skittered away.

"Rags!" he screamed. "Here, boy – c'mon, Rags!"

There was no answering bark, and Sally remembered and silently blessed the cocoa the creature had lapped. Panting, she looked down at Shaw.

"Is my dad in there?" she demanded. The old man showed his teeth in a snarl.

"Find out," he spat. She turned from him, twisting the knob and flinging open the door.

A wave of warm, reeking air engulfed her, but it wasn't that which made her gasp. She'd expected flowers – fragile, exotic blooms whose loveliness would seem incongruous here, but as her eyes adjusted to the light, she found herself looking through a chicken-wire screen at a roomful of bats. They hung from the screen like torn umbrellas, and from the forest of dead boughs propped at various angles across the room. They wheeled and fluttered on the hot, moist air and hauled themselves jerkily across the filthy floor like rats on crutches. And they gathered in a black, heaving mass on something which slumped, strapped to a chair in their midst.

"Dad!" There was a flimsy door in the screen. Sally tore it open and crossed the room, ducking and weaving to avoid branches, the soft collision of furry bodies, the caress of leather wings.

"Vampires," she sobbed, "not orchids." She'd never seen a vampire but she knew she was right. The way they crawled over Dad, jostling one another, feeding on his—

She'd almost reached the unconscious man when she heard a sound behind her. She whirled. Shaw must have retrieved the key, because he'd reached into the room and was closing the door. With a cry of despair she ran back, heedless of bumps and scrapes, and flung herself at the door, grabbing its edge as it swung to and wrenching it from the old man's grasp.

This time it was she who fell, diving headlong through the doorway, and before she could rise he was standing over her with a rusty cutlass.

"The Navy's here!" he cackled, raising the weapon high above his head. Desperately, Sally rolled. The whistling blade chopped the floor where she'd lain. Shaw, wild-eyed, jerked it free and came at her again. "Go on!" he screeched, "Roll! You'll not dodge me for long."

This time she didn't roll. As the cutlass swung up she hooked a foot round his right leg and whipped it from under him so that he fell heavily on his back.

Sally was first up. If he'd lost the cutlass she'd have grabbed it and finished him. She would, but he hadn't. He'd kept his grip on it and was now rising, murder in his eyes. Sally turned and fled for the stairs.

She had no plan. How could she have? Snowbound, miles from anywhere, just herself and a madman with a cutlass. All she could think of was getting out of the house. She must find help for her family, but first she must get away from Shaw.

Bounding down the creaky stairs, she ran along the hallway. She could hear him coming after her. How far behind? Would she have time to turn the key, draw the bolts, grab her shoes – or would he strike her down as she attempted these things?

The shoes weren't there. No doubt Shaw had removed them last night, knowing the Teals wouldn't be needing them again. So it's barefoot through the snow, Sal, if you don't die first.

The lock was old but not stiff, and the key was in it. As she turned it she heard his shuffling footsteps, his rasping breath. There were two bolts, high and low. As she stooped to the low bolt, the cutlass hissed over her head and thudded into the door. Its edge dug into her shoulder as she stretched up to draw the high bolt, and when Shaw pulled it free it cut her. The door was heavy and her wound stung painfully as she pulled it open. A small avalanche of snow toppled over the threshold and she was out, wading thigh-deep through moondrenched drifts with the air like knives in her lungs. And behind her, laughing maniacally, came Shaw. He was old, but he had the advantage of footwear and Sally needed every ounce of her strength to maintain the small gap which lay between them.

She was making for the road, praying that the car was not totally buried, hoping the moonlight would show it to her. An idea had formed in her mind. Not a good one, but the only one possible in her desperate situation. She would lock herself inside the car, switch on all the lights and lean on the horn. Nobody would see the lights or hear the horn because there was nobody, but the glare and the noise might scare off her pursuer. Oh, it was crazy, she knew that. It was far more likely he'd smash all the glass with the cutlass and stab her to death where she sat, but what else was there? In socks and indoor clothing she'd not outrun him for long, and the end would be the same.

She was tiring. At every step a numb foot, deep in creaking snow, had to be dragged clear, only to sink again. Her sodden jeans were plastered icily about her legs and her lungs burned with every inhalation. The road was before her but there was no sign of the car. The old man, endowed with the strength of the insane, was closing the gap.

It was then she saw the light. A slim pencil swinging down the sky somewhere away to her right. Gasping and sobbing she altered course towards it. Shaw must have seen it too because he uttered a string of foul curses as he plunged after her.

She knew what it was of course – what it must be – though she hardly dared let herself believe. A vehicle. A vehicle climbing, its headlight aimed briefly at the sky. It wasn't there now but there was something else – something better, which drew from her harsh sobs of thankfulness as she plunged on. It was the sound of a motor – a whining, struggling motor but a motor nonetheless, and where there's a motor, there's people. She was laughing and weeping at the same time as she waded on and the sound grew more distinct.

She became aware of a pulsating glow, and a flashing yellow light appeared, rising out of the snowdunes. This was followed by the roof to which it was fixed, and seconds later the snowplough's headlights hit her. Its startled driver saw a figure in a thin, bloodied shirt, and behind it an old man brandishing what looked like a sword. He threw the motor into neutral, spoke tersely into his radio and swung down from the cab in time to catch the exhausted girl who flung herself on him.

It was two-thirty a.m. and Dad was dead. Sally could scarcely believe it – wanted desperately not to – but it was true. The plough had been followed up by a police van and an ambulance. A policewoman and a paramedic had beaten off the gorged, sluggish bats and made a rapid examination of their victim but it was too late. The thing which had been a healthy man was now a husk – a bloodless corpse beyond help. They laid him on a stretcher, covered him with a red blanket and carried him down to the ambulance.

Now the house was empty except for the bats and a sleeping dog. Old Shaw was locked in the van and his surviving victims, unconscious still but in no danger, lay beside the dead man in the ambulance. Sally, temporarily bandaged and with one arm in a sling, was walking out to join them, assisted by a solicitous paramedic. A police sergeant was getting into the van. Sally called to him. "Sergeant?"

The man turned. "Yes, Miss?"

"What'll they do with the old man?"

"Put him away for good I should think."

"And what about Rags?"

"The dog, Miss?"

"Yes."

"We'll send the RSPCA up. They'll take care of him." He smiled sympathetically. "And you, Miss – what will you do?"

Sally shook her head. "I know what I'd like to do."

"What's that?"

"Go back to yesterday, when a boring Christmas at Gran's seemed like the worst thing in the world."

The sergeant nodded. "You'll find it hard to believe right now Miss, but this – all of this – will fade with time, and you'll have lots more Christmases, and some will even be merry."

"Merry?" Sally looked at him. "I hope you're right, sergeant, but if not I'll settle for boring."

"There are worse things, Miss."

"I know."

CHRISTMAS PAST

David Belbin

ate on Christmas Eve the motorway was empty but for a white BMW doing ninety in the fast lane. Therese Mortimer drove carefully, keeping her eyes on the road rather than the shadowy Pennine hills. This was a part of the country she loathed, but her stay with Sir Ronald had been worth the drive north. He'd promised Therese his support when he retired, at the next election. Therese, he said, would be the perfect candidate. She was intelligent, attractive and, already, Britain's youngest Euro MP.

"Your local background won't hurt either," he said, though that was something Therese preferred to play down.

"Pity you're single," Sir Ronald added, patting her knee. "Now, if I were a few years younger . . ."

Inwardly, Therese grimaced, but she smiled ingratiatingly at the elderly MP. She was thirty-three years old. Her ambition was to be the country's second female Prime Minister before she was fifty. Therese Mortimer MP wasn't going to have any man sharing the credit for *her* achievements. Not when she'd got so far without . . .

Her thoughts were interrupted. Something was wrong with the car. The engine noise was changing from a low purr to an intermittent rumble. The lights on the dashboard began to flicker and fade. This is ridiculous, Therese told herself. I'm driving one of the most reliable cars in the world. How can it go wrong at a time like this, in such a godforsaken place? Then the engine died. In the moment before the lights went out, Therese spotted an exit road coming up on her left. She swung the wheel round and the car drifted off the motorway. Slowly it slid downhill onto the grass verge, where it would be safe. At least the brakes worked. Therese hadn't been forced to leave the car on the hard shoulder, where someone was bound to crunch into it.

Breathing deeply, she looked around for a signpost, so that she could tell the breakdown service where she was. There wasn't one. Annoyed, she picked up her car phone anyway. They'd have to find her somehow. And when she got back to Essex, she'd give the garage *hell* about . . . but this was the final straw! Her car phone wasn't working either. She knew that it ran off the car battery but it was *meant* to have a rechargeable back-up. She tried again. Nothing.

Groaning with frustration, Therese got out of the car and began to walk down the slip road in the pitch black night. She wished she'd brought a heavier coat. There'd been some talk of snow. Therese found that hard to believe. It hadn't snowed at Christmas since she was young, barely a teenager. But it was certainly cold. She felt something moist brush against her cheek. The first snowflakes were falling. She checked her watch. An hour before midnight. It might be a White Christmas, after all.

There were lights in the distance, but still Therese could find no sign to indicate where she was. She walked on, expecting to come to a roundabout, instead finding a narrow country lane. Perhaps the slip road hadn't been an official exit. Still, she had no choice but to keep going. Slowly, she walked towards the distant lights. The snow fell ever more thickly around her.

By the time she reached the village, Therese's coat was soaked through. The place looked familiar, but she had no time to think about that. It was just another decrepit Northern town full of back-to-back terraces. There were still ancient cobbles on the side roads. Street lamps cast a ghostly amber hue over the grey buildings. She had to find a phone box. Therese turned a corner and found herself in the village square. Maybe here . . .

Recognition hit her like a kick in the stomach. She knew this place. She'd been here before. In fact, she'd been born here. It was called Hebblethwaite. All right, thought Therese, no reason to panic. At least I know where I am when I call the breakdown people, and . . . if I remember correctly . . . yes, there it is – a phone box, one of the old-fashioned red ones. I won't stay here a minute longer than necessary. I'll make the call then hurry back to the car. Before dawn I'll be safely tucked up in my own bed.

Therese picked up the phone and began to dial. It was a real dial, rather than a push-button one. She hadn't seen a dial for years. She pulled out her phone card. Damn! The machine didn't take them. It only took two or ten pence pieces and she had none. The phone gave out a number unobtainable tone. Probably broken, it was so old. Therese left. She'd have to find another.

Looking around the square, it was amazing how little had changed. There was still a cobbler's and an ironmonger's, just as she remembered. But Therese could see no video shop, no Kentucky Fried Chicken. Hebblethwaite must be the only town in the country that didn't have these. The bus-stop displayed the name of a County Council that had been abolished ten years before. How could that be? And surely that mill should have been demolished by now? It was like being stuck in a time warp.

Then Therese worked it out. Hebblethwaite must have been designated a Heritage village. The EC gave a grant to preserve the character of a village as it had been in earlier years, when mills and textile factories were still profitable. You turned the old buildings into museums and created jobs for local people as guides and curators. Redundant workers were re-employed doing the job they used to do, for tourists to see. It was a useful way of reducing unemployment in depressed regions.

So that was it. The village only *looked* old. It was sure to have moved on. Few would remember what had happened twenty years ago, and those who did wouldn't blame her for it. All Therese had to do was find a modern phone. She crossed the square and turned a corner. She'd remembered right. There was a pub there, but it was closed. She was about to turn back, but felt herself being pulled in the opposite direction, towards a cobbled side street.

For a few moments, Therese resisted. But then she decided to be strong. If she became a local MP there were bound to be invitations to visit Hebblethwaite. Best to lay old ghosts to rest now. She crossed the road and entered

Bright Street. Her aunt's old house was the third on the left. Therese would stand outside it for half a minute, that was all. Then she'd find a phone.

Even here, nothing had changed. The door was still painted that ugly magenta colour and there was a Christmas wreath hanging beneath the knocker. In the window was a small tree and on top of it a plaster fairy. It was far too big, just like the one whose leg Therese broke the day after she came to live here. It was silly, but Therese couldn't resist leaning forwards. Yes, there it was – a hairline crack at the top of the leg. It must be the same one. Yet how, after all these years?

The magenta door opened.

"Theresa!"

A middle aged woman stood in the doorway.

"I thought I saw someone outside. Come on in out of the snow, child. You'll freeze!"

The woman stood in shadow, but she looked terribly familiar.

"I'm . . . sorry . . . to have disturbed you," Therese said. "I was just passing. I'll be on my way now."

"Don't be silly, Theresa. Come inside."

"My name isn't Theresa. It's Therese," she told the insistent woman.

"Oh, Therese, is it? Now that's just a silly notion you got

from your friend Stephanie. But you'll always be Theresa to me. *Come inside!*"

Reluctantly, Therese let herself be bundled into the room. She looked at the framed painting of the waves above the fireplace, the ducks on the opposite wall. There, on the mantelpiece, was a photo of her parents' wedding.

"Theresa. Sit down. You've turned white as a sheet."

She did as she was told. Somewhere outside, bells rang.

"Warm yourself by the fire now, dear. I'll be getting ready for Midnight Mass."

Therese looked up. She didn't know what to say. But somehow words tumbled out.

"Aunt Mary?"

"Yes?"

"How come you're still alive?"

Mary gave her a strange look, then laughed.

"You're not yourself tonight, are you, child? Why would I not be? I'm only ten years older than your mother was when the Lord took her and your father, and she was in the prime of her life."

Therese shook her head in disbelief. Mary kept talking.

"Your mother and I lost touch, like I told you at the funeral. But I can't believe she told you I was dead. We argued about her and your dad moving South. But you're back here now, and I'm going to bring you up as my own."

Mary went into the other room for her coat. Therese heard her bronchitic coughs as she moved from the warm room to the colder one. Quickly, she stood up. Once, she had owned this house, after Mary died. What had happened to it? Did someone buy the place, or had it always been haunted? Shivering with fright, Therese went to the door. She must escape now, before this nightmare got any worse. Now!

There was a tinkle of broken glass. Therese looked round. Her coat had caught the photo on the mantelpiece, knocking it to the floor.

"Theresa! What are you doing? My, you're a clumsy girl! First the fairy, and now . . ."

Her aunt stood in the doorway. You won't get me, thought Therese. You won't! Both of her hands gripped the doorhandle. She expected it to be stiff, but it opened easily enough. Therese ran out into the street, then hurried through the snow towards the sound of ringing bells, towards any place where there might be people, light, safety.

As she turned the corner of Bright Street, Therese slammed straight into a tall young woman, almost knocking her over as she came out of a house.

"Sorry."

Therese looked up at the woman's amused face. It felt strangely comforting to see another real human being.

"Are you all right, dear?"

"Yes . . . I mean, no. I'm not. My car's broken down on the outskirts of the village and I can't find a phone to ring for help. Do you have one that I could use?"

The woman shook her head slowly.

"Phone . . . breakdown . . . I don't understand. Aren't you Theresa Shelton, the poor lass whose parents died in the car crash?"

"Yes, but that was twenty . . ."

"Ah, here comes your aunt. Mary, I think your niece has had a bit of a turn."

Aunt Mary was coming round the corner, a grim expression in her eyes.

"Thank you for catching her, Pat," she said. "Now Theresa, what's up?"

Theresa looked from Mary to the tall young woman, Pat. Only now, next to Mary, Pat didn't seem so tall. Therese looked away from both of them and stared at the window of the house Pat had just left. There was light from a street lamp and Therese could see her own reflection. Only then did she realise what had happened. She fainted, falling onto the snowy ground before either woman could catch her.

The bedroom had a damp, musty smell which seemed to seep out of the green flock wallpaper. There was no heating of any kind. Therese pulled the blanket up over her flat chest and willed herself to wake. This nightmare had gone on long enough. The door opened.

"I've brought you some tea, Theresa. Merry Christmas!" Aunt Mary wore a long blue nylon dressing gown, and had rollers in her hair. Therese took the china cup from the tray. Her aunt frowned impatiently. Therese remembered what she was meant to say.

"Merry Christmas."

Aunt Mary smiled. Therese sipped the sweet tea.

"I don't take . . ."

But then she remembered. She had taken sugar when she was thirteen: two lumps. It was only when she went to live with the Mortimers, none of whom took sugar, that she stopped.

"What happened last night?" Therese asked.

"You got a bit upset, that's all – forgot where you were. Pat from down the road helped me to bring you home and put you to bed."

"I made you miss Midnight Mass. I'm sorry."

"Never mind. We'll go to the morning service. I did think of calling a doctor, only it being Christmas . . ."

"No. I'm OK. Really. I'll get dressed in a minute."

"Would you like your presents before breakfast, or after?"

"I don't mind . . ."

Suddenly, Therese realised that she was very hungry.

"After."

Aunt Mary went back to her bedroom. Therese finished her tea and got out of bed. Slowly, the details of the house came back to her. She looked in the chest of drawers and found her cheap childhood clothes. How dull they'd seemed next to Stephanie's. Now they seemed duller still, pathetic even. Today's thirteen-year-olds wore fashionable clothes, loosely cut, with brand names on the outside. Here were shapeless cotton slacks, frumpy tartan skirts, white tights, blouses with nasty frills and old maid patterns. Therese chose the plainest, least objectionable clothes she could find: blue trousers and a black sweater. Then, with a shudder of horror, she remembered the presents she was about to receive.

Finally, it was time to look in the mirror. Therese saw a thin, plain girl whose eyes seemed too big for her freckled face. Her lank, brown hair fell tiredly around her scrawny shoulders. An ugly mole (long since surgically removed) disfigured the bottom of her neck. In seven months time, Therese would begin her main adolescent growth spurt. She would fill out and grow six inches. But right now she was ugly. The old self-hatred welled up inside her.

Therese heard Aunt Mary's bronchitic coughs from the

bathroom. The full horror of the situation was only just becoming clear. Therese was going to have to live through the very worst period of her life all over again. How had this happened to her?

Downstairs, Aunt Mary spooned thick golden syrup onto Therese's porridge. Therese ate in silence. Aunt Mary ate little, but talked as her niece filled herself up.

"This has been a terrible two weeks for you, Theresa. The accident, and the funeral, then leaving your home and friends to return to a place you hardly remember – no child should have to go through such things. It's been difficult for me too, you know. I didn't tell you this, but I couldn't sleep a wink for three nights after I heard the news. I lay awake all night remembering your mother, regretting all the arguments we had. In the end, the doctor had to give me pills. Though I've stopped taking them now, of course."

Therese poured herself more tea, adding two lumps of sugar. Then she took a piece of toast, which she gave a liberal smearing of butter before covering it with marmalade. She knew everything her aunt was going to say. But there was a difference. Now Therese had the intelligence and experience of an adult woman. Maybe this time she could get Mary to change her mind.

"One thing kept preying on my mind," Aunt Mary went on. "What to do about you. I promised myself that I'd bring you up as my own, give you all the love that only your real family can provide. It'll be hard for both of us at first. My health's never been good and you'll need some time to get used to your new home. But we'll make it, I'm sure."

Therese was sure that they wouldn't. She remembered her aunt's death all too well. When the doctor came he'd told her:

"You mustn't feel bad about your aunt. You certainly mustn't feel that it's your fault. I told her when she came to see me after the accident, 'You've got bronchitis. Your heart is weak. You've got no business trying to raise an adolescent girl.' But she wouldn't hear any of it. Just asked me for something to help her sleep."

As Aunt Mary wittered on, Therese remembered her funeral. She'd been surprised at how many mourners there were: far more than at Mum and Dad's. Therese had stood there with the Mortimers, who were to be her new parents, while people from the village filed by.

"So sorry," they kept saying. "You mustn't blame yourself, Theresa." But she had blamed herself. Oh yes she had.

Mary and Therese saved the presents until after church. Therese attracted sympathetic glances from what seemed like the whole congregation. Even the priest addressed a special prayer for "those who have suffered a recent, tragic loss". Therese didn't remember that from before. Probably she hadn't been listening. Now, though, all of her senses seemed very acute. She wanted to take everything in. She wanted to find out whether this was an hallucination. If it was, she had to work out how to end it.

Walking back to Mary's, Therese listened as the wind whistled through the snowbound streets. Aunt Mary kept pointing out houses that her relatives had lived and died in, then telling her about the people who'd come to offer their condolences in church.

"You see, you might feel like a stranger in this town, Theresa, but you've got a history here. There are families living here whose great grandparents came over from Ireland with your great grandparents. Before you know it, you'll have plenty of new friends."

"I don't want new friends. I want Stephanie."

Aunt Mary frowned.

"Oh yes. Stephanie. The Mortimers' girl. Well, you can stay in touch with her, of course. You can write letters, and you can visit in the holidays. Or she can visit here . . ."

Hard to imagine Steph in Hebblethwaite, Therese thought. She'd never been north of the Trent in her life. In twenty years' time, Steph would be living in New York with a commodities broker.

They arrived back at Mary's house. Now came the part

Therese had been dreading. Mum and Dad had bought her Christmas presents before they died. Therese had to appear pleased as she unwrapped a record by a singer she had once liked and a Marks and Spencer sweater which she knew would be too tight. Stephanie's parents, by contrast, had bought her a gorgeous pair of leather boots. Therese remembered how disappointed she'd been six months later when they no longer fitted her.

"Well, they've got money, haven't they, the Mortimers?" Aunt Mary said, examining the boots with ill disguised distaste. "They must have, if they could afford to pay both your Mum and your Dad to work for them."

"They both work themselves," Therese told her. "He's Managing Director of a publishing company and she's in Public Relations."

"Whatever that may be," Aunt Mary said, sarcastically. "I would have thought she'd be better off staying at home, looking after her children."

"Then Mum wouldn't have had a job, would she?" Therese retorted.

"If Langston Mill hadn't closed down before they left, your mother wouldn't have needed a job," Aunt Mary said, bitterly. "She might have had more children and stayed here. If only your father hadn't been made redundant . . . I told him, we can't have Sheltons going into service in this day and age. Your grandfather would turn in his grave. Do you know what your father said?"

Therese shook her head, though she knew exactly what he'd said.

"We've got to do it for Theresa's sake, so that she can have a future."

Aunt Mary stopped. She seemed to snatch for air. Her eyes widened. Then she began one of her coughing fits. With one hand, she reached for a hanky. With the other, she gestured to Therese.

Therese hurried to Mary's bedroom for her cough mixture. There was a glass beside the bottle which contained the dregs of Mary's dose from the night before. The sight of it filled Therese with dread. She found the measure by the side of the bed and poured the required amount of medicine into the dirty glass.

"You're a good girl," Aunt Mary spluttered before pouring the vile-looking stuff down her throat.

The coughing fit ended. Perhaps now's the time, Therese thought. Strike while she's weak.

"Auntie," Therese said, measuring her words carefully. "I'm worried about your health. It can't be any good for you, all the stress brought on by your having to look after me. And there's another thing . . . I really don't belong here, in Hebblethwaite. I hardly remember the place. Mum and Dad used to talk about it, of course. But they used to say how glad they were to have got away. They didn't *want* me to grow up here."

Aunt Mary's face seemed to harden, but she didn't interrupt.

"When Mum and Dad died, the Mortimers said they'd look after me, adopt me if they could, treat me as their own daughter. Mum and Dad were very close to the Mortimers. That's why they made them the executors of their will. And Stephanie and I are like sisters. But they told me, when they found out about you, they felt they couldn't interfere. What I'm trying to say is . . . perhaps it would be better if I went to live with them, in Essex. I feel I *belong* there."

"You *belong* here," Aunt Mary snapped, "with your kin, in the place where you were born. If your parents hadn't left here they'd still be alive today. Think on that! You don't need these fancy southerners, giving you silly ideas. What was the name you wanted to call yourself when you first came here?"

"Therese."

"*Therese!*"

It had been Stephanie's idea – a way to romanticise her boring old Roman Catholic name. Mum and Dad hadn't minded, but now Mary was scoffing at it.

"You were beginning to think you were French! Give it

some time, Theresa. In a week or two you'll go to school, make friends, settle down. Soon you'll never want to leave Hebblethwaite."

"You're wrong!" Therese began to cry. "I hate it here! You're wrong!"

"Now, now," Mary got a hanky from her bag. "You're upset, that's all. Here." She got out her purse. "Why don't you ring your friend Stephanie, wish her a happy Christmas? I'm sure she's missing you too."

Still crying, Therese took the money and put her coat back on. She walked through the snow to the phone box in the square. Something was happening, Therese realised. She had been really upset just then, as though she actually *was* thirteen again. The last twenty years almost seemed like a dream, even though it was one which ended barely twelve hours ago. Now she found herself missing Steph – not the adult Steph, who she'd hardly spoken to since the Euro elections, but her childhood friend.

"Did you want the phone, love?" A man was holding the door open for her.

"Yes, sorry. I was miles away."

Therese dialled the Mortimers' number as she had done twenty years before. She remembered the conversation well, but, as she spoke now, her emotions churned up in just the same way.

"Thank you for the boots. I'm wearing them at the moment. They're lovely. I miss you all so much. I wish I was there. Not here."

Reassuring voices spoke at the other end of the line. They'd see her soon. Perhaps she could visit at half term. Then Stephanie was brought to the phone.

"Merry Christmas!" Steph as chirpy as ever, forcing Therese to try and be normal.

"Merry Christmas, Steph. The earrings you bought me were great!"

"God, I miss you, Therese. It's so tedious with just the little kids around. And the new couple Mum and Dad took on are so boring."

This hit Therese like a stab to the heart.

"But how *are* you? What's it like living in Heatherthwaite?"

"He*bble*thwaite – it's awful. The accent, you should hear it, like they've all got speech impediments. And my Aunt's house is horrible and damp and she's got bronchitis and I keep thinking that she's going to drop dead any moment. And she insists on calling me Theresa not Therese and introducing me to everyone as Theresa. And I miss you so much, Steph, and I hate it here – I just hate it . . ."

Then they were both bawling their eyes out over the phone and Therese heard Steph's dad taking the phone from her. He began to speak softly to Therese, in the gentle, comforting way he had.

"You might be miserable now but things will get better, even though it doesn't look that way. You can always ring us up, reverse the charges if you like. You mustn't let . . ."

Then the pips went and Therese had no more money. She thought of making a reverse charges call, but there was a queue of people outside who had already seen her crying. It embarrassed her. She hurried out of the phone box and ran across the square, stamping footprints into the virgin snow.

Therese kept running, falling over every so often, until she was nearly out of the village. She stood staring up from the valley to where the motorway would be built, wondering what had happened to the last twenty years of her life. She remembered the things that were going to happen from now on: crying herself to sleep every night in that damp bedroom, going to that awful comprehensive school, where all the other kids took the mickey out of her posh accent. It was no wonder that she'd done what she did.

A feeling of dread came over her. What happened took place so long ago that she'd almost convinced herself it wasn't real. For years she'd felt guilty about it, had woken up in the middle of the night with her aunt's face scorched across her mind. But the memory had faded and, with it, the guilt. When she did think about that last night, Therese could almost convince herself that she'd had no choice. She wasn't proud of what she'd done. The shock of her parents' death might have clouded her judgement, but it had still been wrong.

Now, however, she was thinking rationally. If she was going to do it, it would be best to get it over with quickly. Therese remembered the awful evenings at home with her aunt that January, the plot slowly hatching in her mind. But how could she do it *again*? She considered how she'd end up if she stayed in Hebblethwaite. Even if she managed to pull herself clear, she wouldn't be able to take advantage of the opportunities the Mortimers offered. There was no choice, really. She had to steel herself for the task ahead. You only had one life. It was survival of the fittest. The only crime was getting caught.

Therese walked slowly back to Bright Street. She didn't know why this had happened to her, but maybe she could take advantage of it. If she could just remember some of the things that would happen in the next twenty years, forewarned could be forearmed. She would avoid the few mistakes she had made.

"Theresa, where have you been? Dinner's almost ready!" Aunt Mary had done the full works – turkey, roast potatoes and parsnips, bread sauce, carrots and sprouts. The walk had made Therese hungry and she devoured it all.

Tactfully, Mary didn't ask about her conversation with the Mortimers.

After dinner, Aunt Mary fell asleep in her armchair watching the Queen's speech. The afternoon film was a first showing but Therese had seen it several times since. She left it on anyway. Her mind was focussed on what she was going to do to her aunt. Mary did not have a happy life, Therese thought. And the doctor had said that she might drop dead at any moment. There was no point in waiting until late January, as she had before. Therese remembered reading that suicides were highest at Christmas. Should she write a note? No. She'd got away without it last time. To forge one would be to tempt fate.

While Mary slept, Therese sneaked upstairs and into her aunt's bedroom. It was a dark, cluttered room, but she knew where to look for what she wanted. The sleeping pills were on the dresser, concealed behind a make-up bag. Picking the bottle up with a hanky, Therese opened it and emptied the contents into a bit of Christmas wrapping paper she had brought upstairs with her. Then she went into her own room and hid the little packet in her dresser.

Mary woke a few minutes later. Therese gave her a progress report on the film, though her aunt had only asked about it out of politeness. Therese determined to be really nice to her for the rest of the evening, to make her last hours happy ones. She helped with the washing up and made the turkey sandwiches. Twice she refilled Mary's glass of sherry.

"I'm glad that your walk and phone call seem to have calmed you down," Mary told her.

"Yes," said Therese. "I'm sorry I got so upset earlier."

It was strange how, looking at Mary in the harsh light of her tiny kitchen, she reminded Therese so of her real mother. Mary was overweight, her hair was greying, and that perm did nothing for her. Yet, still, the resemblance was there. Recognising this filled Therese with a kind of sadness. She had almost forgotten her real parents. There was no photograph on display in her Brussels flat, or the family home. The Mortimers had replaced them completely.

At ten, Mary went to bed. Therese stayed up a while longer, watching the news. It was interesting, in a way. Yet Therese barely took in the series of events which she only dimly remembered from the first time round. She was too busy thinking about what she had to do.

Aunt Mary was always asleep by eleven. Invariably, she would wake up with a coughing attack between two and three. It used to wake Therese every night. Mary would have a glass of medicine poured out ready by the side of the bed. She would drink it, then drift off to sleep again. Only, tomorrow morning, she would not wake up.

When Therese reached the top of the narrow stairway

Mary's light was already out. Therese called "good night" but there was no reply. Perhaps the sherry had knocked her out. She brushed her teeth but didn't get ready for bed. She would have to wait awhile, until she was sure her aunt was sleeping soundly.

Nervously, Therese counted the sleeping pills that she had taken from Mary's room. There were twenty-four, the same number as last time. How could there be less? She laid her bit of wrapping paper out flat on the dressing table and began to break the capsules open. There was only a little powder in each, but the pile grew steadily. When she had finished, Therese stared at the poison for a long time. For an instant, she even considered taking it herself, rather than face the next twenty years of her life all over again.

It had not been so happy a life, all things considered. Her new mother and father were wonderful to her, but she was always second fiddle to Stephanie, understandably. There'd been some resentment when Therese did better at school, then went to Oxford while Steph had to settle for Durham. Therese worked so hard to be sure of her First that she'd hardly enjoyed university. Even her success in the Union debates had been more for something to put on her CV than a form of pleasure. Everyone assumed she would go into politics, so she did. Central Office were pleased to have her. The future was bright.

But it had been such a grind: building a reputation, sucking up to anyone who could help her, trooping up and down the country in search of some kind of parliamentary seat. And now, just as she was finally getting there, to be thrust back to square one. What was the point of it all?

Snap out of it! Therese told herself. Don't let your thirteen-year-old brain second-guess your thirty-three-year-old one! And maybe this time things will be better. But not in Hebblethwaite, not with Aunt Mary. Do it! Do it tonight, before you lose your nerve.

The village clock struck midnight. Mary would be sound asleep now. Therese took the carefully rolled wrapping paper and tiptoed out onto the landing. No light came from her aunt's room. With her free hand, Therese gently turned the doorknob. With the smallest of squeaks, she had the door open. It rumbled slightly as she pushed it to, but Mary did not stir.

Therese gave herself a moment or two for her eyes to get accustomed to the light. There was the glass on the bedside table, half an inch of medicine in it. Mary breathed noisily. She started to turn over and Therese froze. Then her aunt settled down again. Now. Get it over with.

Therese crept up to the bed and leant over the table, being careful not to make any sound. She tipped the paper roll so that all of the sleeping powder went into Mary's medicine.

Then she put a finger into the glass and swirled it round so that most of the powder dissolved. She stepped back and breathed a tiny sight of relief. It was only a matter of waiting.

"What are you doing?"

Aunt Mary pulled the light cord and Therese, blinking, faced her aunt in a fully lit room. She could say nothing. Mary stared at the piece of wrapping paper in her hand, then at the glass beside her.

"You were doing something with my drink. What?"

Her aunt was awake now – confused but alert. Therese tried to think of an acceptable lie. There wasn't one.

"I was trying to kill you," she said.

Aunt Mary's eyes widened. Her mouth fell open.

"Kill me?"

"You gave me no choice," Therese's words came out in an angry tumble. "Do you think I could settle for living here when I know what life could be like in Essex? If the Mortimers adopted me I could be famous, successful, I know I could. What would my life be like here?"

Aunt Mary started to say something, but it didn't come out. She spluttered, and began one of her coughing fits. Blindly, she began to reach for the glass by her bed. Therese didn't stop her, but Mary remembered in time. Instead, she picked up the bottle beside the glass, took off the cap, and poured some of the red liquid straight into her mouth. then she lay back on the bed, wheezing. Therese thought of going, running away. But it was no good. Where could she run to, when Mary told everyone what she had tried to do?

"You're wrong about the Mortimers, Theresa," Aunt Mary said, when she had recovered her voice. "They wouldn't adopt you when they knew that you had family still alive. I asked them, believe me. Do you think I really wanted to be saddled with you? They said 'no'. They said they felt they had a duty to offer, since they were all you had, but when they found out about me . . ."

"No!" Therese said. "No! I don't believe you!"

"Believe what you want," Mary said coldly. "But I'm all you've got."

Therese shook her head miserably.

"But they'd still have me," she said between her tears. "If you died, they'd still have me, I know they would."

"You're still in shock," Mary said, gently, "from your mum and dad's death. You've been acting strangely for the last day. Go to bed. Things will look better in the morning."

"No," Therese replied, wiping her eyes. "I'm not going to bed. I can't stay here. I'd rather take that drink myself."

She reached out for it. Mary put her hand in the way. Therese tried to knock it aside but her aunt grabbed her arm.

"You're being a silly, selfish girl. Grow up now!"

"I am grown up!" Therese shouted. "I know what I want!"

She tried to pull free but Mary only grabbed her more tightly. Therese struggled. She wasn't sure how much strength she had as a thirteen-year-old, but it had to be more than this middle aged woman. Furiously, they grappled with each other.

Aunt Mary was almost out of bed now. Somehow, she had forced Therese back.

"Theresa, Theresa, stop this! If your mother could see you . . ."

But Theresa was in a blind fury. Everything had fallen apart. Why did Mary have to wake up? Why did she have to tell her . . .

"Theresa, let me go!"

Therese had grabbed Mary now, and was shaking her. Suddenly, her aunt stopped fighting back. Her body seemed to crumple, and she fell to the floor.

Therese waited a moment, then felt her pulse. Nothing. She'd had a heart attack, as the doctor warned she might. Calmly, Therese took the glass from the side of the bed into the bathroom and washed it out. She returned to the room and once more checked Mary's pulse. Dead. Therese was relieved. This was a better death than sleeping pills.

She would get even more sympathy. And if the Mortimers didn't really want her, too bad. They'd have to take her anyway.

Should she call an ambulance now, or wait until morning? She could say that she heard Mary fall. But suppose, just suppose, they were able to revive her? Best to wait a while. Yet Therese couldn't stay in the house. It was so dank and oppressive. She had to take a walk. That was it. She'd get some air, then call the ambulance.

The snow had stopped falling. Therese walked, as she had before, to the edge of the village. There was no-one about. It was very cold. She couldn't be sure if she was shaking because of the cold or because of what had just happened. Try as she might, she couldn't make sense of it all. It was as though the village had given her a second chance, to see if she would change her mind and stay. But Therese was stronger than the village, stronger than her aunt. She was determined. If she had to do it all over again, she would. And she had.

Somewhere in the distance, a car passed. Therese glanced back. The village lights were nearly out of sight. In front of her, another car passed. Which road was that? Therese didn't think there was anything other than the quiet lane she was walking on. Yet there seemed to be a major road ahead. She kept walking. The road she was on bent off to the left, but on her right was a small lane. She walked up it, past the 'Motorway Maintenance only' sign.

Odd, Therese thought as she continued up the lane, that they've cleared all the snow round here. But then she saw something odder, which put everything else out of her mind. There was her BMW, exactly where she'd left it. There was the motorway beyond, ready to lead Therese back to her real home. Maybe the nightmare was over. Therese felt in her pocket. The car keys were there. She got into the BMW and, to her relief, it started, first time.

As she began to pull away, Therese glanced in the rear view mirror, to see if there were any cars coming. Her adult face looked back at her. She appeared older than her thirty-three years, and very tired. Therese stared at her ravaged reflection. She was past caring what had happened to her, or why. Whatever had happened, it was over. She pressed her foot down on the accelerator.

On Boxing Day, Rob Berry, from Hebblethwaite, went out bird watching with his father. While Dad was using his new binoculars to have a look at a heron by the frozen lake, Rob walked up the service road to the new motorway. He wanted to see if any cars were venturing through the treacherous snow and ice. None were. Rob probably wouldn't have spotted the BMW had it not been for the aerial, poking out above the white mound. Curious, Rob brushed some of the snow away. Then he ran off to fetch his father.

Rob hadn't thought to see if there was anyone in the car, but his dad did. Therese Mortimer was slumped over the wheel, dead. She was not, the coroner observed later, wearing a seat belt. It seemed that she had fallen asleep at the wheel on Christmas Eve and driven off the road. However, the coroner added, the collision with the tree was not what killed her. She had received a severe concussion, and had then slowly frozen to death.

THE FAMILIAR

Susan Price

os Savage was in the living room, performing a simple spell to keep her maths teacher away from school, when she heard her mother's key in the lock. She pushed one more pin through the head of the plasticine figure, and went out into the hall.

Her mother looked round a little wildly, then tumbled the armful of schoolbooks she was carrying onto the hall table. She straightened, pushing hair out of her eyes, turned to face Ros and announced, "You're old enough now to understand about these things. I'm moving in with Mike. You can come with me if you like."

For the next hour, as she moved about the house collecting various belongings and stuffing them into suitcases and holdalls, her mother explained why she couldn't live with Ros's father any more. He was unrealistic. He still thought playing in two-bit bands in back-street pubs, for people who couldn't tell a bum note from a pizza, was going to make him famous. He'd never grown up and she was tired of waiting for him to grow up. He was so selfish. And on, and on, and on.

"I'm going," she said again, when she had all her bags by the front door. "But you can come. I want you to come."

"No," Ros said, turning her back and walking into the living room. On the coffee table, on top of the magazines, lay the plasticine man with the pins through his head. The front door banged, and Ros picked up the plasticine man and twisted his head off.

Her dad came back at one in the morning. He'd been in Lincoln, playing. When she told him, he said, "Gone? She's gone? Why's she gone?" Then he went mad and charged around the house, kicking things and slamming doors, and saying that her mother was the selfish one, always had been, always had her hand out, couldn't understand any kind of happiness except the latest new gadget or fitted bloody kitchens. Ros listened, and almost wished she'd gone with her mother. The thing that hurt most in what they said about each other was that it was all true.

Eventually her father had fallen asleep on the settee. Ros

went to bed, taking the plasticine figure with her. She'd baptised it Mike while waiting for her father to come home. She hadn't decided what to do to it yet.

That had been in November. The next month was miserable. They lived on sandwiches and takeaways, while laundry and dirty crockery piled up around them. Her dad was more restless and fidgety than Ros had ever known him, unable to sit still, watch a TV programme or read a page. He found out where her mother was living, and phoned her almost every night. He'd start by trying to be reasonable, and end by yelling insults down the line. Then he'd phone Gran Savage to go over what had been said again and again. The repetition was as boring as it was painful, and Ros often felt like springing up from her chair, kicking her father hard and screaming the house down. But she didn't. Instead she found her plasticine model of Mike, cut off its legs with a kitchen knife, slashed it in half, and stabbed it until it fell apart, while tears of rage and grief splashed about it. But Mike wasn't affected at all, any more than her maths teacher had been. Either magic didn't work or she was doing something wrong. Her books on magic told her that her feelings were too overwrought and out of control. They needed to be concentrated.

Just before Christmas, her mother phoned while Ros was alone. "How about spending Christmas with Mike and me?" she asked.

"No, *thank you!*" Ros said, and hung up.

Her mother had never made any secret of the fact that she'd left home, and her father shamelessly told everyone – almost boasting about it, Ros thought. As a result, both she and her father received more Christmas presents and invitations than usual that year. People felt sorry for them. Ros cringed at the thought of going to any party and facing all those sweet smiles and polite enquiries about how she was coping. Her father must have felt the same, because he suddenly said, "For God's sake, let's go to your gran's and forget all about it."

So they loaded their presents into the van and drove over to the village where Gran Savage lived. Ros left behind her present from her mother. It was on the hall table, where it had been dumped as soon as the postman had delivered it. Leaving it there had given her a sad pain, but thinking of opening it had given her an angry one, and the angry pain had been worse.

They arrived at Gran Savage's early on Christmas Eve, and even Gran Savage, who was usually blunt and curt, had been gentler than usual, all sweet and softly spoken. The falsity made Ros feel quite ill. She sat on the sofa, listening to all that wasn't being said, feeling angry and sad, and wishing fervently that she could change the way things were. Through the window she saw the elder tree.

A short tree, it spread its branches wide. Black branches against a grey day. She got up and crossed to the window. A tree to be wary of, she knew – a witch-tree. Judas hanged himself from an elder, and witches turned into elder trees when they needed to hide. She'd read a lot about them, and her gran had always taught her that it was dangerous to cut an elder's flowers or berries without asking its permission and thanking it. All trees were powerful magically, but there was a special, sinister power in an elder.

With a glance at her gran and father, Ros left the house and went out into the garden. It was cold, and she dragged her big cardigan around her, sniffing the air. It smelt of Christmas coming – that faint tang of rotting leaves and smoke that comes with the first cold weather of autumn and grows stronger as the holiday approaches.

Ros went to the elder and leaned against one of its black branches. She was wasting her time, she thought: none of her serious magic had worked. The odd wish had come true, but her maths teacher hadn't even been mildly sick, and Mike hadn't fallen under a bus, or broken his leg, or come to any harm at all. She might just as well go back into the warm.

Then she thought of what a miserable Christmas it was going to be. Every little thing they did was going to remind them that her mother wasn't with them, but instead of lying down and crying, they were going to smile, pull another cracker, and offer each other another chocolate liqueur. They were going to smile, pull crackers and eat liqueurs until they all went mad.

Suddenly Ros took one of the elder's branches in either hand, and said, "Elder, Witch-tree, help me." Saying it aloud made her feel foolish, even though there was no one to hear. So she mouthed the words. "*Help me,*" she said silently. Her interest in magic had begun when she'd found that if she wished for something hard enough – until it hurt – the thing she wished for often came true. And silently mouthing the words she wanted to shout seemed to make them more felt. She leaned her forehead against another of the elder's branches and *wished*. "I want Mum to come back. *Help me, Elder*. I want Mum to come back for Christmas Day. *Help me*. Make her come back."

Her eyes screwed tightly shut, her hands gripping the branches until she felt the muscles strain in her arms, she concentrated on her wish until her whole self dwindled into a tiny dot of determination in the darkness behind her forehead.

She concentrated so hard that when she opened her eyes, the world seemed different, as if it had shifted and she was seeing it from a slightly changed angle. The colours seemed brighter and bleaker than they had a moment before, and she wasn't surprised to see another face looking into hers from the other side of the elder. It was hard to remember what things had been like before she'd closed her eyes and, for all she knew, the face might have been there all along.

It was the face of a very young man, or boy. A plain, broad face, with wide, knobby cheekbones, a rather flat nose, and eyes which, because they were so close to her own, seemed particularly vivid – a dark grey mingled with ochre, like a lichen-grown stone. His hair hung to his shoulders and, strangely on such a cold, dry day, it was sopping wet.

Feeling that he was too close, she stepped back so as to see him more clearly. He wore a baggy shirt, fastened not with buttons but with lacings. It was open at the throat, showing his white, knobbly chest; and the shoulders of the shirt were darkened with water, soaked by his wet hair.

The boy's trousers were so baggy they looked almost like a skirt. They were tucked into thick stockings, and on his feet he wore big, ugly shoes with wooden soles. Slowly, it began to seem odd to Ros that he was there at all, in her gran's garden, dressed so strangely and so skimpily for a winter's day. But before she could find a polite way to say any of that, the boy spoke. He said something that sounded like,

"Wha bitha doo-win?"

101

Ros poked her head forward, frowning. "*What*?"

The boy spoke insultingly slowly. "What – be – thee – doin'?"

Ros folded her arms and put up her head. "This is a private garden."

"Tha be tryin' to work a charm," the boy said.

"You're trespassing."

The boy went behind the elder and emerged on its other side, ducking under the dark, bare branches. Ros saw that he limped badly on his left leg, and felt guilty for speaking so rudely. "I be gimpy," he said, as if being lame excused him for trespassing. Ros felt unable to say anything without being unkind.

"Wheer's tha ma gone?" he said.

Ros's ear quickly became attuned to his speech. Her gran spoke rather like it, and she and her father could speak like it when they chose.

"How do you know about my mother?" she asked. Her gran must have been gossiping. God, nobody in her family could keep a secret!

"Tha was wishin' for her back," the boy said.

Ros knew she hadn't spoken her wish aloud. Things began joining together to make a kind of sense – the dark winter's day in the half-dead garden, the cold, the witch-tree and, standing under it, this pale boy, with his odd speech and his odder clothes.

"Why's your hair wet?" she asked.

"I was drownded."

Freezing cold air seemed to gather around Ros and press as close to her as her clothes. Drenched in cold, she stood there, staring. A ghost. She was looking at a ghost. And that meant it was all true – ghosts, witchcraft, everything she'd read. Within the cold she felt there flickered a warmth, a feeling of pure glee. She'd asked for help, and the elder had given it.

Clenching her fists and closing her eyes, she said again, "My mother will come back for Christmas Day."

"Tha mun say 'Gimpy, make me mother come back for Christmas Day'."

With closed eyes, clenched fists and all her will Ros repeated the words.

"And now tha mun say, 'As I do will, so mote it be'."

Ros opened her eyes with another little warm thrill of glee. She recognised that line from her reading. It was what witches said when they made their spells. It was very powerful. She cried out into the cold air, "As I do will, so mote it be!"

Gimpy smiled, and then he wasn't there any more. He didn't fade, or vanish – it was more as if the world had been rearranged so that he'd never been there at all.

Ros went back into the house. On the way she noticed the grain in the bricks of the wall, and the subtle range of their colours from yellow to brown. She saw the green paint bubbling on the drainpipe and flaking to show dark brown, rusting iron underneath. She saw the blackened cracks in the white paint of the back door, the rain-laid dirt smeared over the glass. Everything had the super-clarity of a dream, while the boy under the elder tree had seemed, with his pale face and worn clothes – well – ordinary.

Inside, her gran and father were drinking tea and gossiping about some of her father's old friends. They both seemed relaxed, but her father had that same restless fidgetiness about him, and there was something strained about her gran's manner – a sense of her choosing her words carefully. Not really like her gran at all.

Ros sat down at the end of the settee, and it was then that her heart began to hammer, and she felt little shivers running through her. I've seen a ghost, she thought. Then she wondered if she had, and looked about the room, thinking: I'm seeing this. Why should I doubt what I saw in the yard with the same eyes? But what she saw had that same strange super-clarity: she saw every gradation of colour, every slight mark on the wallpaper, a loose thread hanging from a chair cover. I'll have to wait, she thought, clenching her hands on her knees. If Mum comes back for Christmas Day, then it was true.

That evening the three of them walked the few yards to

the village pub. Any other year Ros would have enjoyed the blind eyes being turned to her under-age presence, and the happy noise and heat. But that year her mother wasn't with them, and she was still being plagued with heightened senses. Every tinkle and thud of music from the jukebox in the pub's passage, every giggle, squeal and squawk from the people around her, pressed on her hearing. Her eyes were filled with light from the tinsel and foil lanterns that twisted and twinkled over the bar, and she was compelled to notice every irrelevant detail: a woman's pale blue eyeshadow, the tuft of hair on a man's poorly shaved chin, the food-stain on the front of another's pullover, the tobacco stains and chipped nail varnish on a woman's hands. It made her head ache, and when her gran left early, to make preparations for the cooking next day, she went with her. Her father, who had fallen in with old friends, stayed behind. Ros looked back as the heavy bar door swung shut behind them, and saw him laughing with wide-open mouth as he was teased about his pony-tail.

It was a long, quiet time after, nearly midnight, when there was a thundering on the front door as if someone was trying to punch a hole through it. Gran Savage frowned at Ros and went to answer it, with Ros following close behind. Outside stood a neighbour, who yelled, "Come on!" before starting down the path, waving his arm at them to follow.

Still standing on the step, Gran Savage shouted, "What?"

The neighbour turned and ran back towards them, shouting, "He's been knocked down! Dave's been knocked down! Come on!"

"Oh God!" And Gran Savage ran straight out into the cold night, without stopping for her coat or even to change her slippers for shoes. Ros soon overtook her, and Gran Savage, roaring for breath, was left behind.

Dizzy on her feet from lack of breath, Ros reached the pub. The crowd outside was too preoccupied at first to notice her arrival, but when she was recognised, they stuck out arms and elbows to stop her getting through. That was frightening. What was she not allowed to see? And she didn't really want to see it. She kept trying to push her way through, and calling for her dad, but truly, she didn't want to see.

"It was a car come round that corner," someone told her – she vaguely recognised the face. "Drunk, must have been. Your dad went up in the air—"

The ambulance was so long in coming and, once they were in it, so long in travelling through the dark lanes to the town and the hospital. Ros's first glimpse of her father numbed her. The white brace round his neck. The red blanket (red not to show the blood?). She kept her head turned away from him after that, her teeth gritted, her heart seeming to beat slowly and achingly against a kind of paralysis. Every cry from her father was like a physical blow. "He'll be okay, love," the ambulance man kept saying, but that was like the smiles around the Christmas dinner table. Dead on arrival, she kept thinking. Dead on arrival. Gran Savage, sealed into her own fear, sat quite apart from her.

But he had been alive on arrival, and she and her gran had to sit in the waiting room, waiting and waiting, and looking at the holly pinned above the reception desk. Even there, with the smell of disinfectant and vomit and occasional squeals of pain – even there they'd put up tinsel and were pretending to smile because it was Christmas. And her own thoughts, which she'd wanted to keep concentrated on her father, wandered about over all sorts of things. If you could hurt somebody by sticking a pin into a plasticine model of them, how could you use the model to make them better? And why was it easier to hurt people than to heal them?

And then the doctor had arrived to talk about head injuries and theatre, and to say that they might as well go home. "Phone tomorrow, about nine."

"And I suppose," her gran had said, "I'd better phone your mother."

Ros's belly griped. She felt sick, cold and dizzy. What had she said? *I want my mother here for Christmas Day. As I do will, so mote it be.*

Gran Savage padded over to the phones and made a reversed charges call to her neighbour Geoff. Then they had to wait again, until Geoff came. He drove them home, seeing them through their door with many offers of help and promises to drive them to the hospital again the next day, or whenever they needed to go. "A lovely man," Gran Savage said, once they were inside, "but I'm glad to see the back of him tonight." She went straight to her chair by the fire and sat, staring blankly in front of her. It was fully ten minutes before she said, "You got your mother's number?"

Ros's heart began to beat faster again. She left the room and slowly climbed the stairs, finding it hard to breathe easily. She was using the slip of paper with the number on it as a bookmark in *Practical Celtic Magic*, and once she'd pulled it from between the pages, she held it for a moment, wondering whether to pretend that she'd lost it.

She went back downstairs and gave the number to her grandmother, then stood in the door of the living room, watching and listening as Gran sat on the phone-seat and made the call, speaking in a voice too flat and tired to be anything but calm.

"Hello? Can I talk to Linda Savage, please? Hello, Linda? Brenda. Sorry to phone you so late, but I thought I'd better tell you as soon as I could. David's been knocked down."

There was a faint squawk from the other end of the

phone, which made Ros's stomach cramp, as if she was going to be sick. She turned back into the other room, unable to bear listening to her gran's voice shake, unable to bear thinking of her mother hearing the news and perhaps not caring very much. She closed the door and moved as far from it as she could, hugging herself because she felt so cold. She turned the fire up as high as it would go, and knelt in front of it.

Her gran came back in. "She's coming as soon as she can pack a few things."

Pain spread through Ros, aching in her chest and her head. Her wish was coming true. Would her dad die to pay for it?

Her gran had seated herself by the fire and was once more staring in front of her at nothing in particular. She was prepared to sit there and wait, apparently, until the hospital phoned or she had to get up and let Ros's mother in. Ros went over to the window, pulled the curtain aside and pressed her face against the cold glass, so that she could see beyond her own reflection. The elder tree was invisible, black in the darkness.

"Gran?" she said after a while. "Is this house haunted?"

"Oh, for God's sake, don't start that silly talk! And come away from the window. Stop letting the heat out."

That ended that conversation. There was no possibility of bringing the talk round to the elder tree and its ghost.

It was about breakfast time that Ros's mother arrived, knocking urgently. Neither Ros nor Gran Savage had been to bed. Ros left the chair in which she'd been dozing uncomfortably and went, her face feeling white and numb, to open the door. She turned the knob and walked away, leaving her mother to push open the door herself. Ros didn't feel up to greetings.

Linda Savage marched up the hall, dumped her bulging flight bag on the living-room floor and looked round expectantly.

Gran Savage pushed herself up from her chair. "I'll make some tea. Do you want anything to eat?"

Conversation, over a breakfast of tea and toast, was stiff and formal. Linda asked for another account of the accident, and one was given, briefly. She asked what the doctors had said and was told, even more briefly. "I've got to phone at nine," Gran Savage said, pulling a face. "Christmas Day."

Ros said nothing and ate nothing. Her stomach was too unsettled for her to eat. She sat looking at her mother, at her curly, shoulder-length hair and face made up for some Christmas party. She wore jeans and a jumper, but long, shiny earrings still dangled from her ears. It's your fault, not mine, Ros suddenly thought, with relief and glee. I made the wish, but it was because of you I made it.

At nine, Gran Savage phoned the hospital. Ros and her mother stood near her listening as she said, "Yes . . . Yes, I see . . . Yes, I understand . . . Yes, thank you." Ros wanted to snatch the phone from her.

Gran Savage put down the phone, and had some trouble keeping her voice and face under control. "He's out of theatre. They think it went well. But he hasn't come round yet, so they don't know."

"Can we go and see him?" Linda asked.

"This afternoon. But only two of us . . . I'll go and ask Geoff if he can take us." And Gran Savage went out of the front door without her coat.

Linda turned to her daughter. "You went yesterday, so I'm going," she said.

Ros turned her back and walked into the living room.

Gran Savage came back to say that Geoff would take them, and then they had to wait until it was time to start out. It was a long, dreary wait, with hardly any talk. They did discuss which neighbour should come in to 'sit' with Ros while they were away, but Ros put an end to that by insisting that she would rather be alone. "What do you think I'm going to do? Play with matches?"

They lapsed into silence again, and it was a relief when Geoff knocked at the door, and Gran Savage and Linda rose to go to the hospital.

"Look after yourself!" Linda said, and Ros's face tightened with anger.

"Don't worry – it'll be all right," her gran said fatuously.

The door closed behind them. "Happy Christmas!" Ros said to the paintwork.

Alone in the silent house, Ros sat by the fire with one knee folded under her, staring blankly at a frightening future.

Then, without thinking about it, she rose and went through the kitchen and out into the back garden.

The cold was sharp, but she wouldn't go back inside for a coat. Cold seemed a small thing to suffer while her father was in hospital. She stood hugging herself in the middle of the garden, not yet allowing herself to look at the elder tree. The grey December light spread over the brown fields beyond her gran's fence, and from a neighbour's house came a faint, jingly sound of music playing.

The elder tree at the edge of the lawn was thick, black and old. Its blackness seemed to make the air around it greyer and colder. "Gimpy?" she said, and hoped that she was being foolish.

He was standing by the elder tree. He had been standing there all along. The sight of his thin white shirt, and his soaking, dripping wet hair, made Ros shiver. The wind didn't move his shirt or hair. She took a step closer and stood looking at him for a moment, then slowly reached out a hand and made herself touch him.

She expected to touch another solid human being, because that was what her eyes saw. At the same time, she expected her hand to touch nothing but air, since she'd always understood that ghosts had no substance. Instead, she found her fingers sinking into something that felt like slightly warmed wall-paper paste. She snatched her hand back, resisting the impulse to wipe it on her clothes, and held it away from her. She looked at the thing, with its dripping hair, and its loose shirt which wouldn't flutter in the wind, and she said, "My mother's come."

A smile came to its face. "As tha will, so mote it be."

"Did you make the car hit my dad?"

It still smiled. "Tha mother wouldn'ta come for less."

"And my dad – will he die?"

Gimpy looked at her. Water from his hair ran down his face, dribbling past his grey, stone-and-lichen eyes like tears. "*My* dad died."

"But will *mine*?" Ros cried, her fists clenched.

Gimpy leaned against the elder. "Me dad had eight sons," he said. "The eighth, he was the babby. The seventh, he was special. I was sixth, and gimpy."

"But will my dad die?" Ros said.

"Me dad said, 'Come for a walk with me.' We was by the

113

brook. He took me by the scruff and dowked me head under the water, and drownded me."

Ros shut her mouth and listened.

"He copped me last breath in a bottle, and he put it back into me, and cut his own wrist and dripped blood in me mouth. He buried me under here—" His hands touched the branches of the elder tree. "He called me out when he wanted me. I haunted folk for him, and stole for him, and I went under the earth for him, to ask the dead his questions."

"He was a witch, your dad," Ros said, and, when he nodded, "He made you his familiar." She'd read about familiars – *spirits attendant on, and obeying, witches.*

"He died," Gimpy said. "His last breath went loose – where it blowed him, I dunno. I couldn't follow him. I bain't dead. Bain't alive, bain't dead." He limped around the elder and emerged from beneath its black branches, staring at her. "I'm hungry."

"Will my dad die?"

"My fairther drownded me. Dost think I care for thine? . . . I'm hungry."

Ros stood silent, realising that it was asking for food. "You eat?"

"Drink. Blood." It stared back at her.

"And if – I give you blood?"

"Then I'll follow thee, I'll be tha servant – and tha fairther'll live."

Without hesitation, she held out her arm – but then drew it back. "He'll be – well? Not crippled? Not a cabbage?"

The familiar glared at her, with its stone-grey, ochre-flecked eyes. "Dead or alive?" it asked, like the old game her father had played with her when she'd been small.

"Alive," she said, and held out her hand, the inner wrist, with its blue veins, turned uppermost. Gimpy came from the tree, took her wrist in the soft grip of both his hands, and lowered his head. She felt the bite of his teeth – sharp, yet not sharp enough to hurt – and then she felt a chill even colder than the wind, followed by a curious flush of warmth, and little dizziness, before Gimpy raised his head. His mouth was bloodied with her blood.

"Now if my dad isn't well," she said, "I'll lay you the cruellest way I can." She found herself looking at the wintery garden, where no Gimpy had ever been.

She went indoors, where it seemed hot, so chilled was she by the wind and blood loss. She washed her wrist under the tap, wondering whether to put a plaster on it, but there was hardly anything to be seen – two small raised lumps, like flea-bites. So she didn't bother with a plaster and went into the main room, where she sat and waited, in a state of blankness, for the telephone to ring.

When it did, and she answered it, she heard her gran's voice wobbling near to tears. "He's woken up, your dad! He isn't out of the woods yet, not by a long chalk, but they say he will be okay. Isn't that good?" Ros murmured something. "We'll stay a bit longer and then we'll be home. Isn't it good? Don't worry!"

Ros went back into the other room and sat by the fire. After half an hour, when it was darker, she said, "Gimpy?"

Gimpy was sitting on the hearth-rug as if he'd always been there. "We've made our bargain now, haven't we?" She hadn't read all those books on witchcraft for nothing.

"Blood for service," he said.

She looked at her wrist. "What if I didn't give you any more blood?"

"I'd kill," he said, "whatever thee loved."

Ros nodded. She sat in silence while the room grew darker still, and the strange thing on the hearth still sat there. She asked "Gimpy, could you make mum *stay*? Alive," she added hastily, "and happy. And everyone else alive too, and happy."

Her familiar nodded.

And once that had been arranged, there'd be other things. What was a bitten wrist and a little blood lost every day? She could wear a wide bracelet. And take iron supplements. Power had to be paid for. It was worth it.

THE OLD CORPSE ROAD

K. M. Peyton

t started snowing as they drove North. Not steadily, but in flurries, coming and going.

"I hope this isn't going to be a mistake," Mary Ballard said. "Up in these mountains, snowed in for Christmas."

"Peace and quiet, just us four. That's the point, surely?" her husband answered. He smiled happily. The girls in the back exchanged smiles.

"No Gran, no Uncle Arthur! No sick-making Stephanie and yukky Marie-Claire! It's a great idea, Dad!"

"Christmas is the only time we see our relations!"

"One time too many, Mum. Sorry," said Anna.

"Really, you're too intolerant! Christmas is all about

117

making people happy. It makes Gran happy to see all her family round her at Christmas."

"The trouble is it doesn't make us happy," said Sarah.

"No, well, that's not the point." But their mother didn't continue the argument. She too was ready for a quiet Christmas – no squabbling, no criticism of her cooking, no Arthur getting drunk and trying to kiss the girls. "It might be too lonely, that's all. Two miles up a track to nowhere."

"You can walk over the top and down the other side," said her husband.

"And what's there, if you do?"

"A lake. A road that stops. Nothing else. No Sainsbury's."

"Marks and Spencer's?" Sarah asked.

"We're leaving all that behind."

The thought made Bob Ballard, a mountain man, deeply happy. He hoped to get some decent walking in. All day on the mountain tops and home at dusk to a great feed – the car boot was crammed with turkey, pork, mince pies, cake and goodies – it was his idea of bliss. The girls weren't bad walkers, but his wife hated it. She had brought the tapestry she wanted to finish. Sarah was hoping there might be a pony to ride.

"They're wild up there," her father told her. "Fell ponies. Perhaps the farmer has a tame one you can borrow."

"I hope this farmer will have lit a fire for us."

Mary Ballard looked out across the darkening afternoon landscape and shivered. It was bleak over Shap and the snow was now lying in patches on the tops, outlining the horizon against the sky. She was thinking it would have been nice to have been booked into a cosy hotel down by one of the lakes, rather than into a do-it-yourself cottage up on the moor. She could picture the warm reception, the decorations and the festive dining-room . . . at least the cottage had electricity, the man had said. Her husband hadn't even asked.

They drove on, stopping to look at a map once or twice, and eventually left a narrow road heading up a valley to follow a private farm road. There was a gate to go through, and then it was low gear, climbing, the laden car touching bottom once or twice over the pot-holes. Eventually lights gleamed ahead, and they drove into the yard of a large farm. It was dark by now, and they were tired of the journey. Anna felt a bit sick. Dogs barked and through an open barn door they could see cows on their steaming winter beds, eating hay. A man came out of one of the barns and came up to the car. Bob Ballard wound down the window, letting in a blast of freezing air and flakes of snow.

"You found us then?"

"Yes. We've had a good journey."

"You've just beat the snow nicely. I'll get you the key. All you have to do is follow the track on up – it's a couple of miles. Everything is in order. The wife went up and lit the fires earlier on and there's electric blankets on the beds. You should find it all in order. Anything you want, just let us know."

"That's great."

They took the key and continued their way. There was nothing to be seen but bare moorland on either side, no woods or cosy valleys with tinkling streams. In the last dramatic light of the day, a flare of yellow and orange over the left-hand horizon, they saw their cottage silhouetted, bleak on the skyline. Mary Ballard shivered violently but said nothing. The track stopped at its gateway.

"Well, this is it."

No one made a move to get out, the car suddenly feeling very snug and familiar. The cottage was foursquare, back to the hillside. It had old barns making a yard on the downhill side, and beyond was a gate leading out on to the moor beyond. A light shone in one of the downstairs windows.

"Away from it all . . . I'll say?" murmured Mary Ballard. She laughed suddenly. If not, she thought, she'd have burst into tears.

But Bob backed the car up to the door so that the opened boot stuck into the porch, and they all piled out and got busy exploring and unpacking. The cottage was warm, fires lit in the kitchen and the low-ceilinged parlour that led out of it, and holly decorating the mantelshelves. With the lights on and the food piling up on the kitchen table, it all started to take on a quite different festive look. Once the door was shut the massive stone walls blocked out the snow and the wind and the sour black sky, and their doubts were forgotten. Anna and Sarah ran up the narrow, twisting staircase and bagged their beds, feeling the warmth purring up through the patterned duvets. The tiny windows looked out on to pitch black night. Anna pulled the curtains across sharply.

"You'd never guess . . ." A London girl, the wild outside and the loneliness of this cottage appalled her. Yet she knew in the morning, if the sun shone, everything would be different. People had lived here for hundreds of years, lived and worked and carried their provisions up the track they had bumped up in the car. As their gran kept saying, "You youngsters don't know you're born today!" The wooden stair-post was smooth and shiny with the hundreds of hands that had gripped it coming up and down – people's hands from centuries ago. It made her feel a bit queer. She was the imaginative one. Sarah, two years younger, just laughed.

"I wonder if there's a ghost?" Anna murmured. "Think what's happened here . . ." People dying . . . how far away would the doctor be? He would come on a horse, through the snow and the wind. But now, if they were snowed in and something dreadful happened, a helicopter would come. Nothing was dangerous, or exciting, any more.

"You do look queer," Sarah said.

Sarah had no imagination at all.

After supper they played Scrabble. Mary Ballard was happy now, seeing that the cottage was clean and warm and the oven worked and the gas cylinder was full and the beds were aired, and Bob Ballard listened to the weather forecast and heard that tomorrow would be fair and fine, with snow later. He would get his first walk in. When they were ready for bed, there were stars to be seen and the snow had finished. Anna went outside, to see.

There was an almost full moon and the moors were sharply etched, with deep shadows drawn in their craggy faces and in the clefts where the cold streams ran down. The wind had gone and the air was still and glittery, sharp as needles. Anna went to the gate that led on over the top. Beyond it she could see the thin path scored across the grass. A finger post stood by the gatepost. She could read what it said by the moonlight: The Old Corpse Road.

An uncontrollable shiver made her legs go weak. She leaned over the gate. The farmer had never said anything about corpses.

She went in and told her father. Her mother and Sarah were in bed; he was just going up.

"Yes," he said. "That's the name of this track. They used to bring the bodies along it, up from the lake, to bury them in consecrated ground beyond the valley, where we came up. I didn't like to mention it in front of your mother."

"What bodies?"

"People who died, on the other side."

"Past this house?"

"They rested here, I think."

"You should have said!" For some reason she felt very agitated.

"It doesn't frighten you, surely?" Her father laughed. "The address of this cottage is Deadweight Farm, The Old Corpse Road. Good, eh? But I thought it best not to say. It's a pack-horse road. They carried everything on ponies."

He had done the booking. None of them had known the address. He put an arm round Anna and gave her a friendly hug. "You're not going to have bad dreams, I hope? I like a bit of history, myself. These wild places were more inhabited in the old days, you know – people coped with hardship. All these old ruins you see, they were occupied up until the last century. We'll walk out in the morning and you'll see how lovely it is."

Anna went to bed and snuggled down gratefully into the

warmth. She slept heavily, waking once to hear a horse whinnying somewhere out on the moor. She remembered that there were wild ponies, and that Sarah would be asking the farmer in the morning if there was one she could ride.

The next morning was bright and clear. Anna felt quite differently about the place. It was the day before Christmas Eve, the presents were stacked round the small tree they had brought with them, and their parents were in a holiday mood, all the trouble of the preparation and journey behind them. Bob Ballard was going for a walk over the high ridge above the farm and suggested to the girls that they did an easy walk, following the Old Corpse Road down to the lake and coming back the same way. In the bright morning the name of the track was just a joke.

"You can't get lost. The path is marked with stakes, for when the snow is deep. You won't miss it."

"Can I go down and ask about a pony first?" Sarah asked.

"Yes. I'll run you down in the car and we'll see."

They went down together, while Anna and her mother made sandwiches for the day's walking. But the farmer said he hadn't got any ponies and there weren't any in the area.

"They never come this side of the moor, the wild ones. Never have done. And nobody keeps 'em nearer than the trekking centre down the valley – that's more than ten miles away. If you'd asked, I might have borrowed one for you for the holiday."

"Oh, no, it doesn't matter. Don't worry. She'll have to use her own legs."

They drove home and reported.

"But I heard one whinnying in the night," Anna said.

"You can't have done."

"Well it jolly well sounded like one." But Anna wasn't going to argue, anxious to be off. The sun shone out of a clear blue sky and the snow patches glittered as if sewn with diamonds. Bob Ballard struck off for the highest point above the farm house and the two girls set off up the track. It was easy to follow and after about two miles of fairly easy climbing they came to the point where they could see across to the far ridge. Below lay a serpentine lake, bending out of sight in both directions between the spurs of steep crags. It had a small island of pine trees and the water was very blue, reflecting the sky. There was no sign of life or habitation but the path led down invitingly.

"Let's go down," said Sarah. "We can walk by the lake. It looks really beautiful."

Anna glanced at her watch. It was only eleven o'clock.

"Okay. But we must remember it'll take longer coming back. We mustn't risk getting caught out in the dark."

"It's such a lovely day. And there was a huge moon last night."

They both felt full of go and the valley below seemed to beckon, so pretty and sun-filled, quite different from the wide bleak valley on the other side. The path now left the wide saddle of the moor and plunged down precipitously, twisting between outcrops of rock. It was well-trodden and there was no fear of losing it. Halfway down it converged with a stream running down to the lake, and from there on it followed the stream bank, descending in a series of zigzags, with precipitous drops on the edge, plunging down to the crashing stream below. As they descended they lost the sun, and a mist started to filter up from the lake so that the landscape below became hidden from view.

Anna stopped and consulted her watch.

"It's going to be a fair old climb back up. Perhaps we shouldn't go any farther."

"But we're nearly down," Sarah protested. "The lake is only just below us."

"But you can't tell," Anna protested. "You can't see it."

"It's only a mist over the water. The sun is shining through it – you can see. It'll be clear as a bell at the bottom."

Certainly the air was filled with light, in spite of the mist. When they stopped there was nothing to be heard, no birds, no sheep, nobody. Although their father had said there was a road, there was no sound of any traffic. Anna remembered, without fear, that this was the way they brought the bodies up from the valley, to be interred over in the big valley to the south – but what a climb it must have been!

"They must have used ponies," she said.

"What?" Sarah was curious.

Anna did not reply. And then Sarah was running on down the path and she followed, although her instinct was telling her they should be starting back. And Sarah was right and quite suddenly the mist gave way to bright sunshine, and there was the road below them, and neat little fields beside the lake with a cluster of cottages, a church and what looked like a pub. It had a sign swinging over the door.

"Oh, great! We can get a drink and a hotdog or something!" Sarah had already scoffed her sandwiches and the thermos had only held one cup of tea each.

"We mustn't stay long!" Anna warned, but her heart had lifted at the tranquil scene. There were no cars about, nor any farm machinery – only a couple of carthorses in one of the fields, and a black Fell pony, very shiny and fit-looking. Sarah stopped to speak to him.

"Isn't he gorgeous?"

"He's got a white star and a white sock," Anna pointed out. "Fell ponies aren't supposed to have any white."

"It makes him prettier."

"He wouldn't win at a show! Come on, if we want a drink. Perhaps the pub does coffee."

They were under age for drinking. The place seemed very dozy, with no one about. Filled with curiosity, they went into the pub. They found it extremely spartan, with no tourist furbelows, no pool table or gaming machines, no flock wallpaper – only peeling whitewash and a strange old advertisement for a farm sale. It was empty. They went to the bar and waited, but no one came.

Anna was suddenly uneasy.

"We've no time to hang about. I think we ought to start back."

"Don't be daft!" Sarah shouted "Cooee!" in the direction of the kitchen. "Anyone in?"

There was a sound of shuffling footsteps and a man appeared in the doorway. He was dressed in rather strange clothes and had dirty long hair hanging over his ears. Anna didn't like the look of him at all.

He said, "What are the likes of you doing in here?"

"We want a drink," Sarah said boldly. "Coffee, if you have it."

"Coffee?" He looked blank.

"Lemonade then."

"We sell ale."

"Ale?" Sarah glanced at Anna, not sure what ale was. Newcastle Brown? Lager would be preferable.

"Leave it," Anna whispered.

"Is that all? Only ale?" Sarah did not want to be put off.

"Only ale?" the man repeated sarcastically. "What more d'ye expect in an ale-house? Lasses like you should be at home."

Sarah thought he was mental. Anna kicked her ankle and hissed, "Pack it in, Sarah."

Sarah shrugged and they went outside. It was a relief to be out in the sun again.

"Poor man," Sarah said. "He's a nutter. The landlord should keep him out of sight – he's bad for trade."

"You shouldn't say that. He can't help it."

"I was really looking forward to a drink. Water'll have to do."

There was a pipe running into a trough in the field where the Fell pony was, so they drank there, and went back the way they had come to where their path left the valley road. The path looked very steep, climbing up into the mist that still hung in the cleft. They started up, and were soon struggling.

"We were daft to go right down! I told you so," Anna said crossly. "We're not fit for this sort of thing."

"Dad always says 'take it steadily, slow but sure.' Not like a bull at a gate. At least we're not lost," Sarah pointed out. She was always the optimistic one. She set her face to the path and started to walk with short, even steps, trying to get into a rhythm. It helped. The steeper the path, the shorter the step. No stopping. Head down, heels down, picking the best way. The mist closed round them and the stream roared below in the gradually dusking cleft.

"There's hoof-prints," Sarah remarked. "Perhaps someone rides that pony up. Wish it was on our side of the ridge – it's too far to come over here every day for a ride."

This is the way the corpses came, Anna remembered – no doubt draped stiffly over just such a pony, ankles roped to hanging wrists under the pony's belly. What a struggle! And the mourners slipping and sliding in front and behind. When she paused for breath, she thought she could hear the ghostly clink of iron shoe on rock, a loose stone falling. She stopped. A whinny came faintly through the mist. It must be from below, but it sounded ahead of them. The mist deludes, she thought, and there could be an echo in this strange cleft. There certainly was a pony up on the moor somewhere, whatever the farmer believed. She had not imagined the whinnying in the night. She looked at her watch. It was hard to tell in the mist whether it was getting dark, or just an illusion. There seemed to be no coming out of it this time, and below there was no longer any suggestion of sunlight. It was dark below, and dark above.

Sarah, sensing it too, called down, "What's the time?"

"Just gone three."

"Oh, Lor' – I hope they don't worry about us! We're nowhere near the top yet."

Anna, keeping cool, called out, "We can't lose the path, not with the stakes."

Not to panic. The weather had deteriorated, there was no doubt, the mist coming down with the onset of darkness. But the path was still clear enough. And the whinny came again, quite definitely ahead of them.

"Hear that?" Sarah shouted excitedly. "My pony!"

"It must be one of the wild ones."

Funny the farmer had been so sure there weren't any. Anna peered ahead but could see nothing beyond Sarah's hunched shape, a darker shape in the darkness. There were no stars, not even the suggestion of a horizon. But the sound of the stream was growing fainter and the steepness of the path becoming less severe. Soon they would be out on the moor and over the top. Her anxiety lifted slightly. It was all in the imagination, corpses included.

Suddenly there was a rattle just above them and a dark

shape crossed beyond the dark shape of Sarah. Sarah screamed. Anna stopped dead, heart pounding.

"What is it?"

Sarah gave a sort of sob, and stopped herself. In a low voice, very controlled, she said, "I think it's that pony we heard. God, it gave me a fright! It went across the path. Sparks went up from its shoes. I saw them."

"Wild ponies aren't shod," Anna said, but low enough for Sarah not to hear. She climbed on to come up with Sarah, who had stopped, shivering.

"It's all right. Ponies won't hurt. It might be that one from below, got out."

"It couldn't possibly be ahead of us. It never passed us. There's only this one way up."

"Ponies don't hurt," Anna said again, to convince herself. Why were they so jumpy? It was to do with the mist, and the grimness of the cleft they had climbed up. But they were emerging now, out of the stream valley and on to the open moor. Anna thought she could see the shape of the horizon ahead, and even a friendly stake. Once they got to the top they would see the lights of their cottage. Deadweight Cottage. She almost laughed, remembering. They hadn't told Mum and Sarah the address.

"It's okay, Sarah. We've done the worst."

"That thing scared me."

"I thought you doted on ponies?"

"It wasn't real," Sarah said. "Not a real pony."

"Whatever do you mean?"

"I saw it," Sarah said. "Its eyes. It wasn't real."

"Don't be so stupid!" Anna said sharply.

"It's still there. Listen."

Anna stopped, not meaning to humour Sarah. But she couldn't help it. Quite clearly then she heard the drumming of hooves, not clinking now, but hooves on turf, ahead of them. And the whinny came clearly, and a shout following up. She thought it was a pony got loose, and someone trying to catch it. But there was nobody up here. In her heart Anna knew that.

The mist was patchy, coming and going, but now they were on the top they were out of the shadows of the cleft and the full moon, although hidden, gave a tenuous light across the moor. It was enough to see the stakes by, and the trodden way of the path. But as they walked they were both aware, although neither said, of a presence with them, of something in the edges of the mist, disturbed.

Anna tried not to think of what she knew, walking head down, eyes on the beaten thread of the path. If you let your mind loose, you could frighten yourself. She was sweating with the climb and hurrying now, anxious for the lights of the cottage. But the mist came down again all round them. In front of her Sarah stopped.

"Listen!"

Quite close they could hear the tearing noise of an animal grazing. They stood huddled together, tensed up. And suddenly on the path ahead of them, coming at them, was a black horse galloping. They heard shouts but there was no one there. And the horse did not see them, although it had eyes as bright as stars and its breath was white in the cold. Sarah screamed and flung herself aside and the horse passed like a cold wind, not veering in its path but wildly galloping back the way they had come. They heard the striking of its hooves on rock and, again, an echoing whinny.

"Oh, God, what is it? It's not real, it's not real!" Sarah screamed.

"Oh, shut up!" Anna snapped. "Of course it's real! It nearly knocked us flying, didn't it?" She was shaking just as much as Sarah but knew she must hold out: it was no place to have the hysterics, not now, not sure of the path and the right direction. The way the horse had come . . . she knew that was the right way.

"Come on, hurry up! We're nearly home. Mum and Dad will be terribly worried. A loose horse is nothing to do with us. It's gone now."

"The first time," Sarah gibbered, "it had something on its back. Did you see? But this time it didn't. I think someone's out there trying to catch it."

"It's not our problem."

"It looked like that pony by the pub."

"They all look the same, Fell ponies."

"It had a white star."

"Oh, how could you see, stupid? Pull yourself together!"

"It was dreadful!"

"I thought you liked horses?"

"I hate this place!"

"It was you who wanted to go on – that's why we're stuck out here, idiot! Hurry up now. We'll see the lights of Dead— of the cottage on the top of the rise."

Never had two miles seemed so far, even when the moon came out and they could see home below. Their father came out to meet them and when they saw him coming they forgot their fright. Even Sarah laughed and said, "It was a bit out of proportion up there. Don't tell him."

Was it? Anna could not make up her mind. When they were back home and found it was only half past four after all, not midnight, and their parents had only been mildly worried ("It's a good path. You couldn't possibly get lost, only if the visibility was really bad") it all seemed a bit chastening, that they had been so frightened. They passed it off. ("There was a wild pony up there. It gave us a bit of a fright.") Bob Ballard had had a marvellous day on the high tops and was in a very good humour.

"Lucky, because the weather forecast is bad for tomorrow. Better again on Christmas Day but heavy snow Christmas Eve."

"That's how it should be," said their mother. "As long as we're not marooned."

"The farmer's only got to drive the tractor up. They have snow-plough attachments in places like this. Funny you saw a pony, after he said there weren't any."

"It had shoes on. I don't think it's wild," Sarah said. "Perhaps we could look for it tomorrow."

"Poor thing," said their mother, "if it's going to snow."

"We could track it if it does."

Sarah did not say any more about their experience and Anna decided to keep her fears to herself. It was easy to see how one could panic, lost on an unfamiliar moor, and in panic, a form of hysteria, one could believe anything. She felt slightly ashamed. She slept deeply that night and heard nothing.

The next day it snowed heavily in the morning, as forecast. The girls helped make stuffing and mince pies in the kitchen and their father cleared the snow from the car, and after lunch suggested a short walk up the track to the top, just to clear the cobwebs. "See if we can find your pony. I thought I heard a whinny when I was in the yard."

Anna wanted very much to find a real pony, to prove she

wasn't a hysterical nitwit. With their father everything was different. They got their boots and muffled themselves up and went out up the hillside. The snow came in squalls on a flying wind, sometimes cutting visibility to almost nothing, then suddenly clearing and opening up patches of blue sky. It was invigorating, heady, and they laughed a lot and fell about and threw snowballs. But when they went over the top mist lay below, and out of the wind all was suddenly still and quiet. They could not see the lake, nor the tumbling stream, only hear its distant echo between the rock walls.

"Listen!"

They all stopped.

A faint whinny, far below. A stone falling, bouncing down, making a hollow rattle over the crags, and then, slightly nearer, the whinny again. They all stood frozen, staring down. The trembling fear of the previous evening flooded over the two girls, the atmosphere of the place gripping them with unease as it had the day before. Something evil seemed to emanate from the dropping path.

"There's something there," their father said.

He was not immune, they could see – not laughing any more. They stared down. The mist cleared, and there was a black pony below them, climbing up, head down. It was struggling, as if it carried a heavy load, yet it was a wild one, a Fell pony, with mud in its mane and tail. It came up through the mist and the three of them stood watching, like zombies.

Sarah whispered, "We must catch it!"

The pony stopped and looked up. It tossed its head, showing a small white star. Sarah went down, as if drawn, not saying anything, her boots making no noise. The pony did not turn away. It stood watching, until Sarah reached it. Anna, somehow, expected it to vanish as Sarah stretched out her hand. She remembered Sarah shouting, "It's not real! It's not real!" and the same thought was in her head now, watching. Yet Sarah put the rope she had brought round its neck and came back up the track, panting, smiling, delivering her prize.

"Look, my pony! My Christmas pony!"

They all laughed, the tension breaking apart. Anna found she was almost crying with relief. It truly was a lovely black Fell pony, just like the one they had seen in the field. It *was* the one they had seen in the field.

"It's been out all night! It must have followed us yesterday – oh, how it frightened us!"

They stroked it and patted it and it nuzzled them and seemed perfectly docile on its home-made halter.

"We must take it home, just for tonight," Sarah said. "*Please*! Then we can take it back to its owner when the weather clears."

"We certainly can't take it down this path now. Look, the snow's starting again. We must get home."

"There's a lovely stable back at the cottage. I had a good look round. And lots of straw and hay in the barn, for the sheep. We can make him really comfortable." Sarah was over the moon with her capture, her Christmas made.

They climbed back up over the top and across the moor as the snow started to fall in earnest. Anna felt deeply relieved, all her creepy fears dissolved in the solving of this very simple puzzle. They must have been batty last night, to be so frightened. The pony was as quiet as a kitten and came with them without any sign of unease.

When they got back Mary Ballard came out to laugh at Sarah's magic Christmas present, and they all made up the empty stable with thick straw and put the pony in out of the cold wind. Sarah gave it half a bale of hay and they found a bucket to fill with water. The snow swirled round the barns and the moonlight came and went and the stars flew about amongst the clouds. The pony tucked its nose into the hay and they left it with the sound of its contented munching in their ears. Shutting the heavy door against the night, the cottage was warm and snug and their adventure had given them great spirits, and large appetites.

"It will be fine tomorrow and the hills will look wonderful," Bob Ballard said. "This is what I call a good Christmas."

The wind dropped and it snowed heavily all the evening, but when it was time for bed the sky was clear. The snow lay deep, but there was no more to come. The moon bathed the white hills with a serene light. Before they went to bed they went out to say good night to their pony. The snow was nearly up to the top of their gumboots and they made a deep trail across the yard. The pony was looking out over the door, eating a mouthful of hay, not fretting at all.

"He knows how lucky he is, meeting us," Sarah said, and she kissed him goodnight. As they went back to the kitchen door, he whinnied after them.

The night was fine. Both Anna and Sarah woke up once or twice, excited with the old Christmas excitement, looking forward to their presents. Then they slept heavily, and were woken by the noise of a tractor coming into the yard below. They leapt out of bed and looked out of the window. It was the farmer come to clear a path for them. They went down and the farmer came to the door, shouting, "Happy Christmas! I come up to throw some hay out to the sheep, and show you you're not marooned, like. It's not so deep that you can't get down if you want. Everything okay, is it?"

"It's wonderful!"

They asked him in. Mary Ballard had already made a pot of tea and the table was set for breakfast.

"We found a pony!" Sarah told him. "We put him in the

stable last night. He was lost up on the top there and we brought him down."

"You never! There's no ponies round here."

"Honestly, yes. We'll show you."

"I never seen no ponies round here."

Anna and Sarah got dressed hurriedly and put on their coats and boots. The trail they had made the night before from the kitchen door to the stable was still there, and there was another trail from the door to the tractor which the farmer had made. Otherwise the snow was untouched. It was almost too bright to look at, the sun shining strongly as it rose over the moor.

Sarah ran ahead to the stable and looked in.

There was no pony there. The stable was quite empty.

"He must have got out!"

"He can't have. The bolt is still across," Anna said.

"Where is he then?"

"He must have flown," the farmer said.

The girls were bitterly disappointed. They stood dejected, looking across the bright snow.

The farmer laughed and went back to his tractor. "You'll have to go and hire one at the trekking centre. You can give 'em a ring. We've got the number at home."

He backed out of the yard, and stopped again to unload the hay and throw it out to the sheep waiting over the wall.

Bob Ballard said quietly, "He was right, you know – your pony's flown. Have you noticed?"

"Noticed what?"

"How did he go?" Their father's voice was very strange. If they didn't know him, they would have said he was frightened.

"There aren't any hoofmarks."

Anna suddenly felt very sick. The untrodden snow was so bright that it hurt.

"Ask him – ask him before he goes," she said to her father.

"Ask him what?"

But Anna was already stumbling across the yard to where the farmer was cutting the string on the hay bales.

He grinned at her. "You been drinking last night, is that it?"

"No. We went over the top, my sister and I, and down to the lake, and we saw the pony in a field down there. By the pub. We went in the pub for a drink. And the pony got out and followed us back up. We heard it whinnying. It was real!"

She heard her voice rise on the last words, as if she was trying to convince herself. Why was she saying this to the farmer? She was so afraid!

And the farmer dropped his penknife and straightened up and stared at her so that she was even more afraid.

"What are you saying?" His voice was rough. "There's no

fields down the other side. There's no pub. No ponies. They all vanished fifty years ago, when they drowned the valley to make the reservoir."

"But we went there, to the village!"

"You're dreaming, lass! There was a village, a pretty little village, and a church and a pub, but now they're all under the water and no one's seen 'em since. Not since they built the dam and raised the level of the water. There's nothing down there now, no buildings at all."

"It was the pony that carried the bodies," Anna whispered. "It ran away and the body came off. They were shouting. We heard them. Sarah said it was carrying something!"

The farmer looked at her curiously.

"You need a good breakfast inside you, and a strong cup of tea, I reckon."

And Anna heard her mother calling from the door, "Come along, breakfast's ready! You'll catch your death out there without your coat! Happy Christmas!" she shouted to the farmer. "What a lovely morning! A happy Christmas to all your family!"

UNSEELIE COURT

Tessa Krailing

ooking back on that Christmas, Paul could never be sure whether what happened was the result of his jealousy, that made him do things he would not normally do; or his fever, that made him see things he would not normally see. Either way, it turned out to be a Christmas he would never forget.

At first it had seemed almost too good to be true when his parents told him they were going to Bermuda for two weeks – second honeymoon, recapture old magic, etc. – and asked him if he would mind spending Christmas with relations in Wiltshire. Far from minding he had been over the moon, because the relations in question were his mother's sister Brenda, her husband Derek and their two daughters, Christina and Anthea. He had been in love with his cousin Christina for nine years, since he was five and she was seven. She didn't know, of course. He had never had the courage to tell her. But now he was older, and they would be together over the festive season, mistletoe in the hall and all that, and who knows what might happen?

Then, the day after his arrival, he had learned something that rocked him back on his heels.

It was Anthea who told him. His younger cousin had always been a thorn in his flesh, mainly because she was far too inquisitive and had almost certainly guessed his feelings for Christina. "She's got a secret boyfriend," she had whispered to him slyly when they met on the stairs. "He must be someone special because she hasn't told anyone who he is, not even me. And he writes her love-notes. I know, because I've seen them. Wow, are they steamy!"

At that moment Paul had suffered, for the first time in his life, a sharp and overpowering attack of jealousy. An only child, he had never had any rivals for his parents' affections. He was used to coming first with those he loved – but not, it seemed, with Christina. Before he had even had a chance to tell her how he felt she had found someone else. Suddenly his legs went weak, his throat became constricted and there was a singing in his ears. He realised Anthea was staring at him and said, "I don't feel so well. I think I've got the 'flu."

And as soon as he had spoken he thought yes, that must be it. That was what was wrong with him. A sudden dose of 'flu.

"I expect it's one of those forty-eight hour bugs that are going around," his aunt said, looking at him with concern as he lay stretched out on the sofa. She turned to her husband. "We can't possibly go to that party, Derek, and leave him alone. Not on Christmas Eve. It wouldn't be right."

"He'll be okay," said his uncle, who had already changed into his best suit. "I got those videos in for him specially. I'm sure he'd rather stay here and watch them than come with us. Wouldn't you, Paul?"

"Much rather," Paul croaked. His throat hurt and his head ached and his legs felt weak and spindly as pipe-cleaners. The last thing he wanted was to accompany them to the annual 'do' at the local Golf Club ('Buffet supper, seven till eleven, families welcome'). Not his sort of thing at all – and not Christina's either, he would have thought. He was surprised she had agreed to go with them.

She smiled down at him, a dream in her skinny black wool dress, black tights and tottery-heeled shoes. "Poor Paul, you must be feeling rotten. Would you like to try my miracle 'flu cure?" When he nodded, not trusting himself to speak, she flicked back her long blonde hair and said, "I'll fetch it right away."

"And I'll fetch my box of tissues," said Anthea, following her older sister from the room.

His aunt still looked uncertain. "Are you sure you wouldn't like me to stay behind and keep you company?"

"Quite sure," he told her. "You go and enjoy yourself. I'll be fine."

He hoped he sounded convincing. It would ruin everything if she insisted on staying with him. He had a particular reason for wanting to be left alone. A truly shameful, contemptible reason.

"Hurry up, Brenda," urged his uncle, impatient as usual. "I'll go and get the car out."

To Paul's relief she went, though reluctantly. He lay on the sofa, listening to the sound of them getting ready, slamming doors, running up and down the stairs. It was raining heavily outside. He could hear it drumming against the windows. A foul night – just the sort of night, he thought gloomily, for committing the kind of foul deed he had in mind.

Christina came back into the room, wearing a long black coat. "Here, Paul. This'll make you feel better." She held out a medicine cup full of a thick brown mixture.

He drained it in one gulp. It had a sickening after-taste, but because it was Christina who gave it to him he tried to look as if he had enjoyed it.

"Poor Paul. I do hope you'll be all right."

But she didn't offer to stay at home with him. Suddenly it occurred to him that she might have an ulterior motive for wanting to go to the party. Could she have arranged to meet her lover there? Again he felt a sharp stab of jealousy and immediately his fever seemed to get worse, sending his temperature soaring even higher.

Anthea burst in. "Here are the tissues."

"Thanks," he said shortly. He found it hard to forgive her for what she had told him. "But I'm not streaming yet."

"You soon will be," she promised.

His aunt stuck her head round the door. "Paul, I've left you a little light supper on a tray. Ham salad and a couple of mince pies. Oh, and whatever you do, don't open the door to anyone. We get a lot of practical jokers around here on Christmas Eve."

"That's true," said his uncle, out of sight in the hall. "They've been busy already. Have you seen what someone has done to our sign, Bren?"

"No, what have they done?"

"Stuck a U and an N in front of Seelie Court. Don't ask me why. It doesn't mean anything and it certainly isn't funny."

Un-Seelie Court? For some reason that rang a bell, though Paul couldn't remember why. Of course he knew how this rather upmarket estate of detached, four-bedroomed houses had got its name, because his uncle had told him. The original Seelie Court had been a big old house that got burned down, and it wasn't until three years ago that the builders managed to get planning permission for this estate. All sorts of snags kept cropping up. Local people were not keen to have it there, said it spoiled the character of the village. Paul was inclined to agree with them, but knew it would be tactless to say so.

Christina turned to the door. "It's true, what Mum said about the jokers. When we've gone you'd better put the chain on. Don't let anyone inside."

"Except the Christmas bull," Anthea said. "You'd better let him inside or we'll have bad luck."

"What's the Christmas bull?" Paul asked.

Christina said, "Just an old pagan tradition, peculiar to this part of the world. You're supposed to let him rampage through the house and do whatever he wants. But I wouldn't, if I were you. It'll only be some idiot from the village, stoned out of his mind."

"Christina! Anthea!" their father bellowed from the driveway. "Are you girls coming or aren't you?"

"We're coming."

As they went Christina threw him a sympathetic smile over her shoulder. But it was not her sympathy he wanted.

150

Clearly she did not see him in a romantic light at all, not the way she saw her secret lover. He felt fiery hot, as if the fever were burning him up.

The front door slammed, the car tyres scrunched over the drive. Then silence. He was alone.

He waited five minutes, just to make sure, then flung off the blanket his aunt had tucked over his legs and stood up. He felt a bit giddy. Too early yet for Christina's miracle cure to take effect. He gave his head a moment to clear before starting up the stairs.

Four bedrooms. His aunt and uncle's was the largest; he was in the smallest, the two girls had one each. He opened Christina's door and stepped inside.

The room smelled of her favourite perfume. He didn't want to switch on the light. It would be a dead give-away if someone came back and saw it from outside. Instead he took a torch out of his pocket – he had 'borrowed' it earlier, from his uncle's car – and switched it on. His heart was beating like a bass drum. What he intended doing was a mean, low-down trick and he despised himself for even thinking of it.

He swallowed hard – his throat was really painful now – and directed the torch-beam on to the bedside cabinet. Surely, if a girl received love-notes from a secret admirer, she would keep them in a private place close to where she slept.

"Throat pastilles," he muttered, trying to convince himself

that what he was doing was innocent, even though he knew it was not. "I'm just looking for throat pastilles . . ."

He tried the top drawer, half-expecting it to be locked, but it opened easily. Inside were tubes of make-up. Cotton-wool. Scissors. Emery board. Spare batteries for a radio. A diary . . .

A diary!

It was one of those lockable jobs, with a metal clasp. Everything was in here, no doubt about it. All her most intimate thoughts. 'Dear diary . . .'

He tried to force the clasp. It stayed locked. He picked up the scissors and tried with those. If only his hands would stop shaking! Perhaps a hairpin would be better than scissors. It didn't take him long to find one.

Aaah!

As it clicked open there was a strange scuffling noise in the roof, but he was too intent on what he was doing even to wonder what it was. All that concerned him at this moment was Christina's diary.

Monday, 21st December:	Afternoon went to park. Saw K but not to speak to.
Tuesday, 22nd December:	Christmas shopping with Mum. Saw K in distance. Paul arrived in afternoon.

Wednesday, 23rd December: Decorated tree. Sang
carols in Square. Paul says
he has sore throat. Hope
we don't all get infected.
Couldn't bear to miss
tomorrow night.

So much for sympathy! He had a sore throat and all she
hoped was she wouldn't have to miss the party. Nothing
about her secret longings, no hint as to how she felt about
him as a person. As a diarist, Christina was clearly no threat
to Samuel Pepys. And who was this mysterious "K"?

Hello, there was a pocket at the back.

He drew out three creased sheets of paper. They were
crumpled, as if they had been carried around for some time
and then smoothed. One glance at the first page . . .
"Dearest Christina, I can't wait to hold you in my arms . . ."
told him that he had struck gold. These were the love-notes
all right. Steamy stuff, according to Anthea.

There was that noise again. Something scampering down
the wall-cavities, a mouse by the sound of it. Funny, you
don't expect mice in a modern house. Except that Seelie
Court was on the outskirts of the village, close to a farm. It
must be a field-mouse on the scavenge.

He scanned the first letter, then read the second more

slowly. Sizzling? To an eleven-year-old like Anthea they might seem so; but there was nothing in them to shock or offend, just a setting down of simple, heartfelt emotion. Reading them, he felt like a snake. A creeping, slithering snake, prying where he had no right to pry. Whoever "K" was – and that was the only signature to each letter – he genuinely loved Christina, no doubt about it, and wanted only to tell her so, not to make demands or extract promises. The last letter finished up: "With luck I'll see you at the party on Christmas Eve. Take care, darling. All my love, K."

So he was right. That was why she had been so keen to go to this party. But why did it have to be so secretive? Was "K" much older than she was? A teacher at her school? A married man, perhaps – even a member of the golf club? That would be pretty scandalous.

Or were they just two young people trying to keep their feelings for each other private as long as possible? One thing was sure, Christina was with him now – and Paul was stuck here, searching her diary for clues like some sleazy private detective.

He became aware that the scuffling noise had stopped. Thank God for that. It was beginning to get on his nerves. He slid the crumpled notes back into the diary pocket, trying to remember in what order he had found them, and set about redoing the clasp in such a way that Christina would never know it had been tampered with. He had just about succeeded when he heard another noise, this time galloping hoofbeats outside on the road. Who in their right mind would be out horse-riding at this time of night? Maybe it was one of those practical jokers he had been warned about. Still holding the diary, he moved over to the window and looked out.

It had stopped raining. The street lamp shining on the wet black road showed him the semi-circle of houses that was Seelie Court, their neat open-plan gardens fronting on to the cul-de-sac. And sure enough there was a horse careering around the central traffic island. A black horse, riderless, its mane and tail flowing. It must have escaped from somewhere. Oh Lord, now what was he supposed to do – dash out into the road to catch it and then ring the police?

No, he couldn't. He was sick. Besides, he was no good with horses. Let someone else deal with the wretched beast.

Suddenly it stopped and reared up, whinnying loudly, right at the end of the drive; then stood with heaving flanks, blowing through its nostrils. He could see the greenish whites of its eyes as it looked up at him. Looked straight up at the window, as if it knew he was there, and impatiently pawed the ground.

That was when the first tingle of unease ran down his

spine. The first moment when he began to suspect that
something was seriously wrong. For one thing, it was so
silent out there. So still. He looked round the other six
houses in Seelie Court and saw that only their porch-lights
were lit. Everyone must be out. Gone to a party, gone to
church, gone to relatives for the holiday, gone to Bermuda
like his parents, gone. He was the only person left in Seelie
Court and a horse with green eyes was looking up at his
window.

No, it wasn't, not any longer. In the length of time it had
taken him to look round Seelie Court the horse had vanished, leaving behind nothing but a cloud of vapour and a
curiously charged atmosphere.

Paul turned away from the window and stumbled back
across the room to replace Christina's diary in the drawer.
His hands were shaking as he did so and he felt worse than
ever, sweating hot and cold alternately. He must be running
a temperature. That might explain the horse: a mere figment
of his delirium. He wiped his forehead with the back of his
hand. If only he had a thermometer . . .

The bathroom. There was bound to be a thermometer in
that cupboard with a red cross on the front. His aunt was a
natural-born fusser, the kind of mother who took her
children's temperatures every five minutes if they had a cold.
He opened the door and found what he was looking for

straight away. He stuck it in his mouth and waited for the mercury to shoot upwards into the 100s. And it was while he stood there, waiting, that he heard the scratching.

Not in the roof or in the walls this time, but downstairs. Scratching and whimpering. Still with the thermometer stuck in his mouth he went on to the landing and listened down the stairs. It seemed to be coming from outside the front door. Something wanted to get in. A dog, by the sound of it.

Now he liked dogs. He was far better with dogs than with horses. He crept down the stairs, holding on to the banister to steady himself. At the door he hesitated. What if this time it really was one of the practical jokers? Don't let anyone in – they had all told him that. He put the chain on, took the thermometer out of his mouth and cautiously lifted the flap of the letter-box to peer out.

Two eyes looked in at him, terrifying close to his. Green basilisk eyes, shot with red, glaring at him malevolently. He dropped the flap and leaped backwards, his heart pounding. If that was a dog it must be a huge one, unless it was standing on its hind legs with its forefeet against the door. But those eyes – had they been human or canine? They hadn't looked like either. Some idiot dressed up in a dog costume? Possibly. But the horse could not have been human. No pantomime Dobbin that, but a living, breathing, sleek-muscled Pegasus.

He glanced down at the thermometer. It read sub-normal.

Not surprising in the circumstances. His forehead felt cold and clammy and his knees seemed to have turned to water.

The scratching became twice as frantic and the whimpering twice as loud.

"Go away!" he yelled. "I'm not letting you in, whoever you are."

Why did it have to pick on him? Why, out of seven houses in Seelie Court, did it have to choose this one to claw the door down? .

Because he was the only person here, of course.

He flattened himself against the wall, out of sight if it should open the flap, and shouted, "You don't fool me. I'm not letting you in, so you might as well give up."

The noise stopped. Silence at last.

Except that he was beginning to mistrust silences. Every time there was a silence there was a change of tactic. Mentally he braced himself for whatever came next. After the mouse, the horse and the dog, could it be the Christmas bull?

No, it was the mouse again. Inside the walls. Except it could not possibly be a mouse. Far too noisy. Rats?

He had to be delirious, it was the only explanation. Could you get delirious on a sub-normal temperature? He put a hand to his forehead and found it was damp with sweat. Lie down. He must lie down. Forcing himself to move, he staggered into the living-room and collapsed on to the sofa. But the rats – mice? gremlins? – came with him, swarming invisibly up and down the walls, in the spaces between the floorboards. Just as well there was no proper fireplace, only a mock wooden affair, shelves around the electric fire. If there had been an opening they would have joined him for sure. The noise was horrendous. Squeaking and shrieking. They sounded more like bats now, racing around, getting madder and madder. He clapped both hands over his ears but could not shut it out.

The video! If he put on a movie he would not be able to hear them. He grabbed the first tape that came to hand and shoved it into the machine, then reached for the remote control, pressed the ON switch and waited for the screen to clear. But it didn't. It kept on being fuzzy and making a noise – the same noise as the creatures in the walls. Frantically he pressed PLAY but nothing happened. No picture, just lines jazzing up and down and the noise getting louder and louder.

He threw the remote control on to the floor and started backing away, out of the room. As he emerged into the hall the doorbell rang and he froze. At least the noise had stopped. Another silence. Another change of tactic?

The letter-box rattled. "Paul?"

"*Go away!*" he screamed.

"Paul, let me in."

"Go away and leave me alone!"

"Paul, it's me. Christina. Please let me in. I don't have my key."

"Christina?" Cautiously he moved nearer to the door. "Is that really you?"

"Yes, of course it is. Do hurry up. It's cold out here."

Waves of relief broke over him. He fumbled with the chain and opened the door. There she stood, in her long black coat, blonde hair gleaming in the lamplight, smiling at him.

"Are you all right?" She stepped past him into the hall. "You sounded most peculiar."

"No – I – well, it's this 'flu bug. It's sort of making me have delusions."

Her foot scrunched on something and she bent down to pick it up. "What's this?"

"Oh, it's the thermometer. I must have dropped it. I was taking my temperature. It's okay, I haven't got one. It's below normal. I think that's why I feel so peculiar." He asked anxiously, "Is it broken?"

She tossed it on to the hall table. "Smashed to pieces."

"Maybe I can mend it."

"Don't be silly. It's beyond repair. We'll have to buy a new one." She took off her coat and hung it in the hall cupboard.

160

He watched her every movement. "Why have you come back?"

"I was worried about you, Paul." She glanced into the mirror, flicked back her hair, and walked into the living room.

He could hardly believe his luck. Christina had come home because she was worried about him! He followed her into the room.

The TV was still on and now behaving perfectly. She glanced at the screen – a James Bond movie, what else? – picked up the remote control and switched it off.

"Sorry I didn't open the door straight away," Paul said, "but I thought you might be another of those jokers."

"Another? Have you had one round already?"

"More than one." He sat down on the sofa before his legs gave way. "They're pretty clever, I must say. So far I've been visited by a black horse . . . and a dog . . . and there've been rats or something in the walls."

Give Christina her due, she did not laugh at him. She would have been perfectly justified in laughing at him, because he must sound like a raving idiot. If it were not for the fever he would never have blurted all this out. But she must have recognised he was not feeling normal because she gave him a long, considering look and said, "Oh, yes. They're clever all right. Fiendishly clever, you might say."

"Who are they, do you know?"

"I've a pretty good idea." She sat down in the armchair opposite him and crossed her legs. Long slim legs in silky black tights. He watched, mesmerised.

"Well – who?"

She leaned back in the chair. "Shape-shifters."

"Shape-shifters?"

"Goblins, if you like. Boggarts. Things that go bump in the night. Have you never heard of the Unseelie Court?"

"Not until tonight, when your father complained about someone changing the sign." But even as he spoke he realised that he *had* heard of the Unseelie Court. His Scottish grandmother – Aunt Brenda's mother – used to tell him stories when he was small about the bad spirits who belonged to the Unseelie Court. That was why the name had rung a bell. And his aunt must have passed the stories on to her daughter. He stared at Christina. "You're not suggesting I've been visited by *goblins*! Oh, come on, I may be feverish but I'm not deranged. This is all a practical joke – right?"

Ignoring his question she sprang up from the chair and went over to the window. "What intrigues me, Paul, is why they picked on you."

"Because this is the only house in the Court that's occupied tonight and I'm the only person in it. At least, I was until you came home."

She opened the curtains a crack and peered out. "So you are. But you must have done something, otherwise they wouldn't be interested in you." She swung round to stare at him. "Something to make them think you'd be an easy target. What was it, Paul?"

"What was what?" He tried to look innocent.

"What did you do that you shouldn't have done? Something mean and sneaky, that made you ashamed."

He swallowed hard. "I don't know. I can't think—"

"Can't you? I can." She came towards him slowly. "I think you read my letters, Paul. My private letters. You wanted to find out who they were from."

His heart seemed to stop altogether. There was a roaring in his ears and his throat had seized up so badly he could hardly speak. "How – how did you know?"

"Oh, I guessed that's what you intended to do as soon as we'd all gone out. Anthea told you about the letters and you were curious. You wanted to know who they were from, didn't you?"

He nodded, speechless.

"And now – are you any the wiser?"

He shook his head.

"No, of course not. You've no idea who K is, and you never will have. That's my secret and I intend to keep it. What a nasty, sly boy you are!" Her voice lashed him with scorn. "How could you ever imagine I'd look twice at a skinny little rat like you?"

It was the scorn that did it. It told him what he might have realised sooner if his brain had not been so fuddled, that whoever was standing in front of him *could not possibly be his cousin Christina*. Christina would never be scornful of him, it was not in her nature. Moreover she was not a mindreader and therefore could not have known that he had read her letters. No, this . . . this *thing* was a shape-shifter, able to take on whatever form it wanted. First the mice, then the horse, the dog, the rats, the bats . . . and now the girl he loved. He stared up at her face and saw not Christina's clear blue honest eyes but the malevolent green ones that had looked at him earlier, through the letter-box.

She – it – went on, "You deserve everything that's coming to you, Paul. Tell me, do you know what happened to the original Seelie Court?"

He said hoarsely, "It burned down."

"That's right. Several times over. Each time they rebuilt it the same thing happened again. Now this estate has been here three years. About time history repeated itself, I think."

It sounded like a threat. If only his brain would clear! He had to think quickly, be cleverer than this monstrous creature if he wanted to stay alive. Frantically he searched his memory for what his grandmother had told him, all those ancient folk tales, trying to recall if she had mentioned an antidote. Something with magical properties, that would drive out evil spirits. But what chance did he have of finding anything magical in this soulless modern house?

Wait! There *was* something in the hall, if his grandmother was to be believed.

"Christina . . ." He managed to make himself say her name, even though it was a mockery. "You're right. I did read your letters."

She smiled, with satisfaction.

Feeling sick in his stomach, he forced himself to go on. "I had to, because I was jealous."

She went on smiling.

"But I'm sorry. And I promise I'll never do anything like that again, if you'll grant me one wish. Something I've wanted for a long, long time."

"What's that, Paul?"

"Let me give you a kiss."

She looked startled; then said, "All right. Just one." And extended her cheek.

"Not here." He got to his feet and took her hand. It was cold and limp, like the hand of a corpse. "In the hall."

"Why in the hall?" Reluctantly she allowed him to pull her through the door.

Not answering, he positioned her exactly beneath the mistletoe. He tried not to let himself think about what he was doing, just in case she could read his mind. But careful though he was, she must have picked up some hint of his intentions because she said suspiciously, "I don't know that this is such a good idea. I might catch your 'flu."

"No risk of that." He kept a firm hold of her hand. "You'll be protected by magic."

For a moment she looked puzzled; then, as if sensing danger, she glanced upwards. When she saw the white-berried bough suspended above her she gasped and tried to free her hand, but Paul hung on grimly, at the same time reaching upwards to grasp the bough. He felt a strange thrumming in his chest, as if a warm current were running from the mistletoe right through his body and into the hand that held Christina's. She gave a fearful, inhuman shriek and pulled away with such force that he had to let her go. At once the thrumming within him stopped, and he felt a surge of triumph. His grandmother had been right! Mistletoe, the golden bough, was the ancient protection against evil.

But his triumph turned to horror as he saw the Christina-thing start to change its shape, metamorphosing rapidly through its previous manifestations – horse, dog, rat – shrinking, shrivelling before his eyes, until at last it seemed to stabilise as some sort of a winged rodent. Not quite a bat, but a hideous, green-eyed creature with hairy webbed black wings which it spread wide and flapped until it took off.

Paul ducked as it skimmed over his head and began to fly around just below ceiling level, uttering shrill, piercing cries. He clapped his hands over his ears to shut out the noise, but it penetrated his brain, making him feel stupid and confused. All he could do was crouch there, watching in horrified fascination as the creature continued its crazy flight around the hall, circling and diving, every now and then swooping down so close it touched his hair. It seemed to be trying to do something – but what?

The answer came as the plugs began to spark. The wall socket, the overhead light – every appliance in the house suddenly became cracklingly alive. Then he remembered what the creature had threatened – to set fire to Seelie Court. And in a house without fireplaces the only thing it could do was attack the electrical system.

Next moment the lights went out, plunging him into darkness. All he could see were sparks and flashes as the wiring short-circuited. Any minute now the whole place would surely burst into flames. In desperation he began to crawl across the carpet towards the front door. He felt the beating of wings as the creature zoomed low over his head but went on crawling with only one thought in his mind – escape. *He had to get out of this house.*

At last he felt the roughness of the mat beneath his knees and the solid oak of the door in front of him. Cautiously he began to clamber upwards until he touched the chain – still off since the Christina-thing arrived – and found the catch. Swaying dizzily he got to his feet, and as the creature swooped again he managed to wrench open the door. Met by a blast of cold air, he reeled back in terror.

There, on the doorstep, stood a man with the head of a ferocious, slavering beast, red nostrils flaring, black eyes glittering, a pair of cruelly pointed horns. He uttered a deep bellow, lowered his head and began to charge.

Then everything went black.

He came round to hear people talking. First, the gruff masculine voice of a stranger. "Poor kid. I didn't mean to give him a fright, Derek, honest I didn't."

"It's okay, Ted." This time it was his uncle who spoke. "Not your fault. He wasn't feeling too good when we left the house."

"That's why we came home." His aunt's hand rested soothingly on his head. "I was so worried about him I couldn't enjoy the party."

He opened his eyes to find himself lying on the sofa in

the living-room. "What happened . . .?" He tried to sit up but his aunt pressed him back against the cushions.

"Best lie still, old son," said his uncle. "You've had a bit of a shock – and no wonder, seeing Ted on the doorstep dressed like that."

Paul turned to look at the red-faced young man holding a papier-mâché bull's head under his arm. Not a shape-shifter, just a normal human being carrying out an ancient country custom.

"But – but the lights—"

"Electrical fault," said Ted. "Fused everything. Good thing I turned up when I did, or you might have had a nasty fire."

"Hear that, Paul?" his uncle said jovially, still in a party mood. "Ted here, when he isn't larking about the country-side dressed as a bull, just happens to be an electrician. Yes, I reckon luck was on your side this evening, young man."

"That's because he let the bull inside, like I told him to," Anthea spoke from behind him, seated on the arm of the sofa.

"We've a lot to thank you for, Ted," said his aunt.

"Aye . . . well, I'd better be getting along." Ted gave Paul a sheepish look. "Sorry if I scared you, son. Hope you feel better soon."

"Wait—" Paul struggled into a sitting position. "It wasn't

you that scared me. You were just the final straw. But before you came there was something else . . . like a sort of – bat."

Ted frowned. "Now you come to mention it, something did fly out over my head when the door opened. Could have been that caused the short circuit, Derek."

"As I said, lucky you arrived when you did. I'll show you out, Ted."

When they had gone, and Anthea had been despatched, despite protests, off to bed, Paul asked his aunt if her mother had ever told her about the Unseelie Court.

She thought for a moment. "No, I can't remember she ever did. *Un*seelie Court? You're confused, Paul. I expect it's the fever."

"She didn't mention boggarts or evil spirits or—" It was no good, he could not bring himself to say the word 'goblins', not while she was regarding him with that kindly but sceptical expression. Anyway, she was probably right. It must have been the fever. The whole thing had been a delirious nightmare. He had never left this sofa all evening. He had dreamed the whole thing from start to finish.

Except that Ted the electrician had seen something fly over his head when he opened the door . . .

Christina came into the room – the real Christina, with her honest blue eyes. "Oh, Paul. You didn't even eat your supper. It's still there, on the tray."

"Wasn't hungry," he mumbled. He found it hard to look her in the face. Even if he had only dreamed all that about prising open her diary and reading her letters, there was no escaping the fact that it had been what he intended to do. Now he would never know for certain if someone called "K" actually existed. What's more, he didn't *want* to know. It was none of his business.

She turned to her mother. "Look what I found on the hall table. It's your thermometer, smashed to pieces. Looks as if someone must have trodden on it."

"Poor Paul." His aunt looked at him sadly. "Were you trying to take your temperature? You must have been feeling bad. Tomorrow I'm going to get the doctor, Christmas Day or no Christmas Day."

"No, really," he protested. "I feel fine now. Honestly. My fever's gone."

And so it had. Miraculously. Along with the soreness in his throat and the flabbiness of his limbs. Gone as quickly as it had come.

"It must have been that 'flu cure you gave me," he told Christina.

"Perhaps," she said dubiously. "Although I've never known it work so quickly before. Still, as long as you've recovered that's all that matters."

"Oh, I have," he assured her. "I've recovered completely."

And not only from the fever, he realised. What was it they sometimes called jealousy – the green-eyed monster? Yes, that was it. He had been cured of the green-eyed monster.

THE ROAD FROM RUSHOUT WOOD

Joan Aiken

n a frosty Christmas Eve in the early years of this century, it was the misfortune of Hugh Tregear, a young gentleman making his way across country on a bicycle, to knock his front wheel against a rock that lay in the road with such force as to render the bicycle temporarily unfit for further travel. The rim of the wheel was bent out of shape, and a blacksmith would be required, or at least a handyman with better tools at his disposal than our young traveller had about him.

Hugh, a student at the University of Cambridge, was planning to spend the Christmas holiday with his sister. Recently married to a clergyman, she had taken up residence in a small village lying some fifty miles to the east, in a part of the country unfamiliar to our young friend, who had accordingly plotted out his itinerary on a map. Consulting this in the fading light, he now found that his nearest hope of assistance appeared to lie in the village of Goose Acre, some two miles ahead of him.

Kicking aside the rock that had done the mischief, and muttering a few uncomplimentary comments about the elders of a parish who permitted their byways to remain in such a state of disuse and neglect, Hugh began lugging his bicycle as best he could along the rutted and stony lane. This task was rendered even more difficult because the forewheel refused to turn at all, and so the whole front portion of the bicycle had to be hoisted into the air. Our traveller was further burdened with a pack on his back, which contained Christmas presents as well as his toilet articles and change of clothes, so that his progress along the lane was necessarily very slow.

Many times he stopped and mopped his brow, despite the white frost that furred the leaves and thorns in the hedge-rows. Many times he was tempted to leave his machine behind the hedge, in hopes of discovering some accommodating person at the next village who might be prepared to come back for it with a horse and cart. But then he recollected that it was, after all, Christmas Eve, and that most of the villagers would, by now, have left their work for the day. He guessed therefore that they might be reluctant to set out again on such a chill, gloomy, and foggy evening. Indeed, he began to wonder if there would be any chance at all of getting his machine repaired at such an hour, on such a day. The prospect of reaching his sister's house in time for any Christmas celebrations began to recede farther and farther into the doubtful distance.

Fortunately for Hugh, this part of the country was at least very flat, and he had no troublesome slopes to contend with. In fact, after traversing a mile or so of scrubby woodland (he recalled that, on the map, this coppice had been named Rushout Wood) the lane began to descend very gradually into a gentle dip, while its banks on either hand rose higher. Our traveller now thought he began to detect the vague outlines of buildings which stood back at some distance on either side of the road ahead, though in the dusk, which was now thickening fast, it was hard to be sure of this.

"It can't be a village," he thought. "Goose Acre must be still at least a mile ahead. But perhaps it may be a large farm with buildings on both sides of the track. And at a farm – especially one of such a size as this seems to be – it is certain they will have tools for mending farm machinery, and perhaps they may be able to help me straighten out my wheel. Though it is odd that I don't remember seeing a farm marked at this point on the map, I suppose I must have missed it in the dim light.

"Phew! I certainly shall be glad when I can stop dragging this heavy bike along."

Before the mishap, he had already been riding for a couple of hours. The encounter with the rock had thrown him to the ground and jarred his shoulder. He began to find himself very weary.

"If the farm people can't mend the wheel for me," he thought hopefully, "at least they might offer to put me up for the night."

And his fancy began to play with agreeable visions of a huge open farm fireplace, thick clusters of glistening berried holly over the mantel, leaping flames, mugs of hot sweet punch, and the cheerful rumble of friendly rustic conversation.

Greatly to his dismay and discouragement, what he now began to hear instead was the distant, angry barking of dogs; more than one dog, Hugh thought – two or three at the very least. Perhaps more. The baying, interspersed with howls and snarls, had a decided note of menace about it. This was not simply the straightforward watchdog alarm signal which warns the householder that a stranger's step is approaching his boundary; these sounds contained a rasping, raging, rattling reverberation which suggested, rather, a savage longing to get at the invader and tear him to pieces.

Hugh had always disliked dogs. They had no charms for him. His family had invariably inclined to cats as pets; he had never engaged in a friendly relationship with any member of the canine tribe. He regarded dogs at best as fidgety, odorous, demanding, unnecessary creatures; at worst they were excitable, nervous, quarrelsome, overflowing with aggression. A disagreeable species rendered worse, in most cases, by their masters.

He stood still, set down the front wheel of the bicycle, and considered, looking about him in the frosty gloom.

The barking ahead of him intensified in volume. There began to be something positively hysterical, frenzied, in its tone.

How many dogs could they have at this farm, for Heaven's sake? And on which side of the road was their territory? And were they tied up or loose?

At this juncture Hugh began to debate in his mind whether it would not be better to turn back. He was no coward, and could have dealt well enough, he told himself, with *one* dog, even if it came at him with hostile intent – but if there were two, or three, or four . . .? His tweed jacket and thin flannel trousers would be wholly insufficient protection against their fangs (and now he could not repress a sharp shudder at the prospect of sharp, dirty teeth gouging into his neck and arms and legs), and he had no weapon with which to defend himself.

Hesitating, he glanced back along the lane, which ran straight as a rule, sloping gently upwards out of the little dell. He tried to recall how great a distance lay between the last village he had passed and the point where his accident had taken place. A mile? Two miles? And he had pushed the bike for at least a mile through the wood. That meant probably three miles before he got back to the village – a grubby, depressed little hamlet called Cropham, where he had briefly considered trying to obtain a cup of tea at one of the cottages before deciding that they all looked too dirty and unpromising. No, there was little to be hoped for from Cropham. And yet, Hugh thought, he had really better turn back.

The baying of the dogs ahead of him was now positively bloodcurdling. But when Hugh looked more carefully along the lane towards Rushout Wood, what he saw there changed his attitude so completely that, regardless of what peril lay ahead, nothing in the world would have made him return along the way that he had come. Any danger from the dogs suddenly seemed a minor consideration.

Rushout Wood itself was now no more than a black mass of furry trees that spread out like a wolf's pelt across the horizon.

Out of the trees, and along the narrow straight road, something was coming at a most unnaturally fast and ungainly pace – something shapeless, oblong, and whitish.

"It is a tree," Hugh thought confusedly at first. "It is the stump of a silver birch that has been shattered in a gale. With patches of white on its broken trunk, and patches of dark."

And then he thought: "No, it is *not* a tree. It is a person."

And then he thought: "*It is putting itself together as it comes towards me.*"

At this point Hugh let go of his bicycle, which fell on the track, and glanced desperately about him for a stick or stake or some other weapon to fight off the dogs. Go back and confront that whitish, patched-together thing with its long thin arms extended in front of it – that he would *not* do, though Cerberus and all the hounds of hell were lying in wait for him at the farm entrance. In fact he could not even bear to look behind him again and see how close the – whatever it was – had come. Snatching up a crooked piece of oak branch, with a few leaves adhering to it, that had fallen from the hedge, he ran on down the road, stumbling in his terrified haste.

There was no chance of climbing the banks – they were now well above his head, and crowned with dark hedges of thorn or holly.

He could not hear any footsteps of the thing behind him – if it *had* feet – because of the yelling clamour of the dogs ahead.

Now Hugh came to a kind of crossroads where, on either side, gated entrances led to the farm and its outbuildings. The gates hung wide open. To the left, some way back, stood the house – a long, low, shadowy building with numerous dark windows and doors, none of them illuminated. The whole place was shrouded in dimness and a garden-patch with rows of cabbages and a large well-head lay in front of it. To the right was a spacious farm yard with cart sheds and haystacks, a tumbril, vaguely seen in the twilight, loaded with something that looked like roots, a path of frosted nettles, and a rusty harrow.

But where, all this time, were the dogs? Were they shut up? Their clamour was everywhere and yet Hugh could not see a single one of them.

What he did see were two men.

They stood on either side of the road, looking at him and at one another, each of them in an open gateway. Their faces were not distinguishable to Hugh in the intense gloom. Here, at the deepest point of the lane, the banks were topped with trees and were twice the height of a man.

Both men stood perfectly still. They did not move. But Hugh received from them such a powerful impression of rage – hate – deadly intent – that it made him tremble. The chill of it was like a knife in his breast.

Words from the Bible came to him: Their faces shall gather blackness.

"I have got to get out of this place, I have *got* to," he thought, "or I'm done for. Either from them, or from what is behind me. And where is *that*? And do they know it is there?"

He felt himself frozen to the stony ground with terror, and with the fury and malevolence that seemed to be all around him. It seemed to him as if the two men had laid a barricade across the road – a barrier of hate and ill will.

"But they can't *do* that," thought Hugh confusedly. "The road is not theirs. The road is the King's Highway. Nobody is allowed to block it. No body."

No spirit?

He knew himself to be in deadly danger – a danger that he could not understand, that surrounded him like a thick and poisonous smoke.

"If I don't leave this place," he thought, "I shall be shrivelled up like a leaf in a fire. I shall be lost. I am very nearly lost already . . .

"I shall fly into fragments like that thing on the road behind me."

He tried to gather himself into a single whole. "I am Hugh

Tregear, from Church College Cambridge, on my way to visit my sister Fanny. I have a lace shawl for her gift, and coral teething-rings with silver bells for the twin babies. I have a book for Tom, my brother-in-law – a book of poems.

"If I could – if I could think of a line from one of the poems . . ."

Then he thought of a line:

Forth, pilgrim, forth! Forth, beast, out of thy stall . . .
Hold the high road . . .

He began to struggle forward, panting, pushing his way with straining muscles and bursting heart through invisible bands of opposition. "They *can't* block the road, they *cannot*, it is the public highway. It is the right of every citizen to walk it unimpeded. Unopposed."

Step by step he forced himself to go forward, with the yelling of the dogs in his ears to right and left. He tried not to look at the two men.

But he was obliged to, for their faces burst into flame. "Their faces shall be as flames," thought Hugh, "all faces shall be burnt therein."

He heard two appalling screams, of hate, rage, despair. But they were behind him.

Then at last Hugh was free and able to run. Sobbing,

gasping, crying out, with his heart rattling against his ribs, he pounded onward.

How far he had run or at what point he fell, he did not know, but there came a moment when exhaustion and terror folded over him and he collapsed into a blank and blessed pit of sleep or fainting, which held him numb and close for many hours.

When he next woke he found, to his amazement, that he was in a bed in a small and sunny bedroom. Not far away he could hear the clamour of church bells.

He pushed himself up, exclaiming confusedly, "Where am I? Oh, my heavens, I must hurry—"

"Now don't 'ee fret, my dear, don't 'ee!" soothed a kindly voice. "Reverind Musson, he be over in the church, a-celebrating the joyful day, and you being safely preserved; but he'll be back pressingly. Do'ee lie down, now, and take a nice drop of tea, that'll do 'e famous good."

The aproned old lady who spoke now limped out of the room, but returned after a moment, bearing the nice cup of tea and a slice of thin bread-and-butter, which did indeed taste like manna and nectar to our young traveller.

"Where am I?" he asked again.

"Why, you're in the Rectory at Goose Acre, my dear, and

Rector hisself he'll tell ye, by and by, all ye want to know. Now just bide ye quiet till he comes."

This Hugh was glad to do. He lay passive in the lumpy, hammock-like bed, watching the mild play of flames in the small hearth, and the rooks circling the stone church tower which he could see through the window. And presently the bells, which had gone silent, rang again in a joyful hurricane of final celebration.

Then there came a step on the stair, and a thin, black-haired man with an intelligent, penetrating face, came into the room.

"Mr Tregear?" said this person. "We are so very glad to see you better."

Hugh was astonished. "How did you know my name?"

"Why," he said, smiling, "I took the liberty of examining the papers in your pocket and found the letter from your sister. So then I took the additional liberty of sending her a telegram to inform her that you had suffered a minor accident but were in good hands here, and would be able to join her later on."

"Oh, sir! Thank you!" exclaimed Hugh, immensely relieved. "She will have been so worried. I *do* feel in good hands – indeed I do! But what happened to me? Where did you find me?"

"You were lucky," said the Rector gravely. "You were

wonderfully lucky. We gather that you had suffered a mishap to your bicycle? and so were pushing it, walking along the lane from Cropham, that runs through Rushout Wood and passes the ruin of Oldhouse Farm?"

"Yes – yes – that is what happened." Hugh was puzzled. "The ruin? But surely – ? In any case, how do you know these things?"

"I had been visiting a sick parishioner last night. I was driving back in my motor car. I saw you lying in a heap at Cropham crossroads. So I brought you home, guessing what might have occurred. And this morning Sam Walsingham, one of my farmer parishioners, went out with a haycart and recovered your bicycle. (We deduced the bicycle from the fact that you were wearing trouser clips.) And of course," ended the Rector obscurely, "there is no danger at Oldhouse in daylight."

"Danger? Then—"

"My dear young friend, are you better? Do you find yourself restored enough to rise and share my Christmas meal? I shall be glad to give you the whole explanation, but I believe that you may sustain it better after some solid food. If what my excellent Mrs Rutter has prepared may be so designated."

Hugh exclaimed that he was well, quite well enough to get up, and would be very happy indeed to get up and share the Rector's Christmas lunch.

185

Eyeing himself in the wash-stand mirror, though, as he shaved, he was quite astonished at the thin, haggard face that looked back at him. It seemed to have aged by seven years since yesterday.

"Now, draw up a chair to the fire," said the Rector, when the festive meal had been despatched, "and I will tell you about the Hernshaw family who lived at Oldhouse Farm a hundred years ago."

"You said ruins just now? Nobody lives there any more? But I heard the dogs barking. And saw two men. And a – and a something—"

"You were fortunate," said the Rector again. "Nobody in this neighbourhood ever walks past Oldhouse Farm at night. In a car, yes, it is safe enough to drive quickly by, or on one of those motor-bicycles. Even perhaps on a bicycle, if one pedalled hard enough and fast enough. But walking is too slow. It lays you open for too long to such terribly malign influences. Especially on Christmas Eve."

"But *why*? What happened there?"

"The farm belonged to a man called Abel Hernshaw, a widower. A surly, sour-natured, ill-conditioned man by all accounts. He had an only son, Mark, who grew up in the course of time, married a girl with some money of her own, and moved to a farm of his own, Cathanger, lying to the west of Rushout Wood. There had been quarrels, tensions between the two men before that, it is said. But all was patched up after Mark moved out; indeed he had a child, Lucy, who was her grandfather's pet by all accounts. A spoiled, wayward little madam, apparently – took after her father and grandfather . . .

"Mark with his wife and daughter used to go over to Oldhouse at Christmas time, to spend the day and eat their dinner with the old man.

"It is known that Abel Hernshaw had a hobby of breeding fierce dogs, collies and bull terriers. There would always be two or three about the place, ready to come rushing out and harry any passer-by who took the road that led through the middle of the farm. In the records of the Parish Council there are various notes of complaints against Farmer Hernshaw from people who had been assaulted by his dogs. But his retort always was that nobody was obliged to go that way, through his farm; if they chose they could take the southerly road from Goose Acre to Cropham, which is only a scant half-mile longer."

"That's true," said Hugh, who had noticed this alternative on the map and rejected it.

"Abel Hernshaw said that he was not going to keep his dogs tied up for any man. The job of farm dogs was to run loose and keep guard over the place.

"Well, one Christmas Mark arrived as usual to spend the

day with his wife and daughter. But this time he also brought along a dog of his own, just as bad-tempered and combative, it seemed, as those bred by his father. And of course there was a battle between his dog and one of Abel's; a window was broken in the scrimmage, and Abel's dog was hurt so badly that it had to be shot. This made Abel so angry that he told Mark never to come back to Oldhouse again. No more Christmas visits. And during the following year Abel got himself several more dogs to replace the one that had been killed.

"The next Christmas Lucy demanded to go as usual to her grandfather's. It seemed that he had always hidden a gift for her in the hay barn, and the spoiled child saw no reason why this practice should have been discontinued, just because her father and grandfather had quarrelled. 'What is that to do with me?' she said. 'I want my Christmas toy from grandpapa. It will be in the haymow.' 'He will not have left it this year,' her father told her. 'And I absolutely forbid you to go there.' But Lucy took not the slightest notice of his interdict. She waited until all the household were busy with Christmas preparations, and then put on her mother's Christmas gift to her – a fur coat made from white ferret-skins – and stole away secretly from Cathanger Farm, through Rushout Wood, and so to her grandfather's place. She did not go to the house, but directly to the hay barn where the old man had always hidden her present.

"And, of course, the dogs heard her."

The Rector paused.

"What happened?" asked Hugh with a dry mouth, although he could guess.

"Why, the dogs went after her. She ran. Lucy must have been a fast runner – she had got as far as Rushout Wood when they finally caught up with her. But then they tore her to pieces."

"And her father? And grandfather?"

"Mark Hernshaw went to Oldhouse that evening, as dusk fell, and shot all the dogs. He took lamp-oil with him and set fire to the building and the ricks. The old man came running out and tried to stifle the blaze with brooms and sacks. Nobody else was there; no one would work for him by now. Mark flung oil over his father too, it is thought, and the fire caught him. The two men struggled together, and finally fell, or jumped, into the well. Since that time nobody has lived at Oldhouse Farm."

"What a dreadful tale," said Hugh. "I saw them – it must have been them – on either side of the road, staring at one another. Hating one another."

Of the tattered, dishevelled, leaping thing that had run after him out of Rushout Wood he could not speak.

I suppose, he thought, she comes back to see her grand-father get his just desserts.

"I wonder how long it will go on, the haunting? I felt such an atmosphere of hate – terrible hate."

"When it is as fierce as that I am afraid it may take many more decades, centuries even, to die away," said the Rector sadly. "I repeat that you were lucky, my young friend – supremely lucky – to escape. Some have not been so fortunate. People have been driven out of their wits, or suffered heart attacks. How – can you remember? – how *did* you manage to fight your way through?"

With reluctance, Hugh cast his mind back.

"I think – I was thinking about the road," he said uncertainly. "Thinking that it was every citizen's right to go along it unhindered. And – to wrench my thoughts away from those two figures and their hideous hate – I was going through, in my mind, the presents for my sister and her family that I have in my pack. I thought of a book – yes, the book I had brought for my brother-in-law, and of a poem in it – Chaucer's Ballade of Good Counsel: 'Hold the high road, and let thy ghost thee lead, And Truth thee shall deliver . . .'"

"Ah, now I begin to understand," said the Rector. "And your Guardian Ghost came, very promptly, to the rescue."

"I – I think so," said Hugh. "Yes."

"And the road, perhaps, played its part. Roads are very ancient and powerful constructs – older than buildings, far older than towns, many of them go back unimaginable distances in time. They must in some way hold the essence of all that has been carried along them. They stand for the connection of one spirit to another, the urge to make journeys and discoveries, the need to move in a forward direction, the need to make pilgrimages. Roads, like altars, have rights which must be respected."

"Yes," said Hugh again.

Mr Musson smiled.

"But now you, my young friend, must be on your own road. My neighbour Mr Whinstone the blacksmith has mended your machine. It is only a scant hour from here to your brother-in-law's parish – you will be there long before dark, in time for Christmas tea!"

"Oh, thank you, sir! You have been so kind—"

"No kindness. A great pleasure. And let us hope that, by battling against it so successfully, you may have reduced the malign power of Oldhouse Farm and made that road less perilous for others. Goodbye, and a safe journey to you."

Hugh thanked his host again, shouldered the pack full of presents, and mounting his mended machine, set off pedalling along the flat, straight road that led from Goose Acre to his sister's village. And behind him the westering sun flung out his long shadow, which ran ahead of him along the highway like a beckoning ghost.

I'LL BE SEEING YOU

Jill Bennett

 eter! Robert! Breakfast!" their mother shouted from the foot of the stairs.

"Must you shout like that?" Mr Hopwood, his foot on the top step, took the full blast.

"I'm sorry, Michael – it may be the first day of the holidays but I've things to do and the boys are still in bed."

"I'm not on holiday – I'm late." Her husband continued down the stairs and swept into the kitchen. "Let them go without, lazy toads!"

"Coming, Mum." Peter appeared on the landing and aimed a thump at the door next to his. A muffled protest answered him. "Can I have an egg?"

"Cook it yourself if you want to, I'm trying to get ahead today. Have you combed your hair?"

"Oh, Mum!" Peter poured a mound of cereal into his bowl and reached for the milk.

"Good morning, Peter," said his step-father with marked politeness.

"Good morning, Michael," Peter replied good-humouredly with matching courtesy.

The boys' father had died when Peter was eight. He was eleven when his mother married again. There was no question of their step-father being called anything other than Michael.

"Christmas!" It came as a long sigh from his mother. She was writing a shopping list on a pad on the kitchen worktop. "Everything's ordered, I've bought the crackers – Michael, have you sorted out with Joanna which day we're having Mary Ann?"

"Christmas Eve, for lunch. She'll pick her up again on Boxing Day."

Peter groaned. "My room again, I suppose."

His mother looked at him. "I thought you and Robert enjoyed sharing last time."

"We had a great time, but – I've got my TV now and . . . well . . . it's different."

"What's so different?" Peter's elder brother said as he

came into the kitchen and pulled his chair out. At sixteen he was lanky and had the overgrown look of a young ostrich. He was very conscious of the fact that his skin was erupting with spots, and that his shaky attempts to shave didn't help. He spent a long time in the bathroom every morning dithering between dabbing on antiseptic or splashing about with a more glamorous aftershave. This morning the antiseptic had won hands down.

"Enter the chemist's shop!" Peter wasn't known for his tact.

One of Robert's toe caps kicked him under the table.

"Get off!" Peter glared at him.

"Boys!" Their mother turned on them, exasperated. "It's Christmas soon, the season of good will, remember? Mary Ann wants to be with Michael this year. She hasn't seen him at Christmas for two years now. She wants to be with her father but she probably wants her mother too. It's a strange time for her and I want her to be happy. It's a pity we can't all get together but we can't, so there it is."

"Good thing," Peter muttered under his breath.

Michael pushed his coffee cup away and stood up abruptly. He knew that sometimes their situation became complicated and a bit tense, but he couldn't cope with it this morning.

"Of all the selfish people you take the trophy, Peter!" His

normally quiet voice was loud and hard. "I agree, it is hard luck on Robert that he has to share his room with you for two nights. Both of you are on holiday now and your mother needs help. Try and think of someone other than yourselves just for a change, can't you?" He went out into the passage to put on his coat. Jane Hopwood followed him.

Peter and Robert looked at each other.

"Big mouth!" said Robert.

Peter was silent. Just recently he always seemed to be the one to stir things up. He never knew how it happened and he hated it. Two Christmases ago, when Mary Ann came for the first time, he and Robert had a whale of a time together. They had thumped each other with pillows and competed to get up the earliest to find their presents. They had never stopped giggling. Now it didn't seem to be so easy. Robert was often rather lofty and superior, which made Peter dig back at him whenever he could get in a good swipe. Like this morning. He sighed.

Their mother came in. "That's a good start to the holidays," she said as she took some toast out of the toaster and brought it to the table.

"Sorry, Mum," Robert mumbled.

"Yeah, sorry," Peter was even more inaudible.

Their mother sat down between them. "All right, we'll begin again. Robert, don't forget your library books have to go back. Peter, you can do a bit of shopping for me. There's not much, and I really think you should be getting your present for Mary Ann before you forget altogether."

"Mum!" There was real agony in Peter's voice. "I thought you were getting one for us."

"Not this year. You're old enough to do things for yourself. Robert's got his for her already."

Robert looked smug. "A book," he said.

"Oh, but . . . Mu-um . . ." The agony was still there, and the face to match.

"For goodness' sake!" His mother rose. "I shall begin to think Michael might have a point if I hear any more of this. There's the list, here's the money. Don't you dare lose it and I want you back by eleven."

Peter headed off for the supermarket with his shoulders hunched against a light sprinkling of rain. They were also hunched against the turmoil inside him. At that moment he could willingly have throttled Mary Ann. He had saved up his weekly money so carefully, budgeting for all his presents and still leaving enough for him to buy the latest hand-held computer game. It had been touch and go, for they were very expensive, and he'd only just got enough. His best friend at school didn't have it yet and Peter was dying to

197

get it first. Now he had to get a present for Mary Ann and he wouldn't have enough money.

"Feeble-minded girl!" He had no idea what an eight-year-old girl liked anyway. In the supermarket he tossed the packets and tins into his trolley viciously. At the bottom of his heart he knew he was being mean and this made things worse. He hated feeling guilty and Mary Ann made him feel guilty. He hated Mary Ann.

Still raging he left the supermarket and headed for Boots, where he wandered around staring at the Christmassy shelves and seeing nothing that seemed suitable. His anger, pent up and frustrated, began to give way to a feeling of misery as he looked bleakly at tins of talcum powder, face flannels and toilet bags. He didn't want to go to the local toy and model shop, which was the logical place, because he couldn't bear the thought of seeing his longed-for game and having to buy something utterly boring for someone else instead.

As he left the shop he let the heavy glass doors swing shut without a backward glance, unaware that they nearly crashed into an elderly lady who was approaching with her shopping trolley. Nor did he hear her mutter angrily as he walked away, heading for the toy shop. He was in such a mood that if a dog had been foolish enough to cross his path at that moment he would have aimed a kick at it.

As he dragged himself unwillingly along, Peter could hear somebody shouting. Turning into the street where the toy shop stood, he saw who it was.

A young man with tangled long hair and a shabby anorak stood beside a sizeable basket full of video tapes.

"Tapes for sale!" he was shouting. "Cheap videos for sale!"

Intrigued, Peter went up to see. There were masses of tapes in a pile and a placard stuck to the side of the basket read "£1.50 each".

Peter's heart leaped. Perhaps here was a way out. If there was something here for Mary Ann, there would still be just enough money left for his game.

"Young man." The salesman saw him approach and dipped his hand into the basket to draw out a tape. "I've just the video for you." He held it up for Peter to see.

The box had a picture of an old man on the front. He was covered in icicles which also formed a kind of spiky crown. "Stories from the Winter King", Peter read. "Tales to enchant for all ages." All ages – that could mean eight. Peter put his hand in his pocket.

"I'll take it," he said eagerly.

The young man slipped it into a plain paper bag and held out his hand. "One-fifty to you, son. Have fun!"

As he put two pound coins into his outstretched hand Peter thought, "One-fifty to everyone, you mean."

As he handed over the 50 pence change, the tape seller looked straight at Peter and said, "Not everyone – just you."

Peter stared. He knew he hadn't spoken out loud, so how did . . .

Still looking at Peter the young man deftly switched the label on the basket over so that it now read, "Tapes £3.50 each." He grinned broadly at Peter's astonished face and added, "'Bye for now. Be good. I'll be seeing you."

A cold finger began to travel up from the base of Peter's spine. Why did those ordinary words "I'll be seeing you" sound somehow, well, threatening? What's the matter with me? he thought.

Then he suddenly noticed the young man's eyes. They were the most piercing blue eyes he had ever looked into. They seemed to shoot their glances right through him in a way that didn't quite go with the grin. Peter shivered again.

"Thank you," he muttered quickly, turning for home.

A feeling of elation grew inside him as he neared his house. He had a really good present for Mary Ann *and* he still had enough money for his game. Everyone would be pleased with him. Even Robert couldn't scoff at it, and if he didn't tell them how much it actually cost they'd have to eat their words about him being selfish. After all, he'd bought super presents for everyone now – in fact he couldn't wait to see their faces as they opened them on Christmas Day.

By Christmas Eve the tree was up and glittering and all the food was in. Peter was helping his mother to roll out mince pie pastry when Mary Ann arrived. Robert was upstairs wrapping up his presents, so it was Michael who opened the door. She got out of the car and hugged her mother while her father took out her little suitcase.

Then he said, "Well, Joanna, a happy Christmas!" and Mary Ann's mother replied, "Well, Michael, you too." They looked a little awkwardly at each other for a moment and then Joanna was in the car and driving away and Michael had swept Mary Ann into his arms and was whirling her around.

Peter and his mother came out of the kitchen to greet her, wiping their damp hands on their trousers.

Jane went forward to give her a kiss and Peter thought, "She's still skinny – and little." He looked at her fair colouring and her hair, worn long and straight, falling in two mousey swatches over her shoulders. She was gazing timidly about and he thought that even her eyes were not quite blue and not quite brown. Suddenly he was glad he'd got her a nice present.

To break the awkward silence, Michael said, "Peter will take your case, darling. Go upstairs with him. You're sleeping in the same room as before."

Inwardly Peter sighed. "My room, he means." But he was resigned to that now. His only regret was leaving the battered old TV set that his grandad had given him for his birthday. He loved the sense of privilege he had as he lay on his bed and watched programmes by himself. Also, better still, Robert had been furious.

"Only two nights," he thought, and as he picked up Mary Ann's case he said, "OK. Come on," and led the way.

Mary Ann was a gentle, quiet child. She was in awe of the two boys and not used to their boisterous ways. His mother kept a watchful eye on them to see they didn't go too far.

They divided the evening between playing games and watching television. Mary Ann enjoyed games as much as the boys. She was very good natured and held her own quite well. When she lost she didn't seem to mind and if she won she didn't crow. The boys warmed to her and Jane and Michael watched her settle in with relief.

In the Hopwood family the children's presents were left in pillowcases outside each bedroom door on Christmas Eve. Stockings were never quite the right shape or size. Larger gifts were left under the tree downstairs, everything to be viewed together after breakfast. The last thing that Jane and Michael did before they went to bed was to tiptoe around with the bulging pillowcases. They knew that the boys were probably listening for any sound.

To his surprise, Peter fell asleep quickly, tucked up in his sleeping bag on a sunbed on Robert's floor. When he woke it was still dark and everywhere that Christmas morning was blanketed with freezing fog. Robert's bedside clock said ten to six. "Presents!" he thought, wriggling out of his warm bed and creeping towards the door. Two bulging bags were leaning against the passage wall. He peered at them and scooped up the one with a huge P pinned to it. As he did so he heard a sound coming from downstairs. It was bitterly cold on the landing – the heating in the house didn't come on till much later – but Peter crept down the stairs to see what was happening.

To his surprise, the television was on. Pushing the sitting room door open, he saw Mary Ann sitting on the floor in front of the set. She was in her nightdress and sat hugging her knees, watching the screen intently.

"You're up early, Mary Ann," he said.

"Shh!" she replied in a whisper. "This is great!"

Peter came and stood looking over her shoulder. With a warm glow of satisfaction he realised that she was watching the tape he had given her, "Stories from the Winter King". A story was just coming to an end and when it had finished the screen was filled with the image of a large jolly man. Unlike the picture on the front of the box he wasn't covered in icicles, but was dressed in a ragged tunic and cloak. His white hair was long and shaggy and mistletoe was wound about a gold circlet on his head.

"Did you like that one, girls and boys?" he laughed, taking a swig from a goblet in front of him. "Keep watching, there's another story coming up. 'Bye for now," and he pointed his finger at the viewer. "I'll be seeing you!"

The Winter King's laughing face filled the screen as the camera came in closer, but Peter shivered. Those were the same words that the young man had spoken as he handed Peter the tape in the street. The icy finger he felt then began to travel up his spine again. Peter watched fascinated as the Winter King's eyes looked into his own. They were such a piercing blue that they made him gasp.

Mary Ann turned round. "Oh Peter," she said, her face glowing, "it's a wonderful present. The stories seem to go on and on. I've seen lots already."

She turned back to the set, unable to tear herself away from the flickering images.

Her happy enthusiasm broke the spell and Peter was

able to mumble something like, "Er . . . glad it's all right . . . um . . ."

This was better than he expected, and his chest swelled with satisfaction. Remembering, he peeped into his present bag and wondered if Robert was awake yet. His feet were going numb.

"It's very cold in here," he said.

"Is it?" Mary Ann was too engrossed to notice.

"Well, er . . ." Peter turned towards the door, not knowing how to go gracefully.

Mary Ann got to her feet with a rush and, leaving the television for a moment, moved towards him.

"I think you're just wonderful," she said seriously, and before Peter could move she put her arms round his neck and kissed him on his cheek.

Embarrassed beyond words Peter stepped backwards and as he did so he caught his bare feet in the edge of the rug, tipping him off balance. His bag of presents shot out of his grasp as he tried to save himself, and he fell headlong, hitting his head hard on the sofa leg.

Darts of bright light exploded behind his eyes as Peter lay still waiting for them to stop. His cry and the noise of his fall brought Jane dashing down the stairs, closely followed by Michael. Mary Ann stood, stricken and silent, appalled by what had happened.

"He just fell over," she said in a whisper. "He just fell."

Peter sat up and began to rub the side of his head gingerly. It really hurt and a large lump was beginning to form under his hair.

"Let me look." His mother bent over him, parting his hair gently. "Oh, nasty!" she said sympathetically. "But no blood, no need for stitches."

Michael turned the TV off. Mary Ann started as he did so, as if she was going to protest, but she said nothing. The room suddenly seemed very quiet.

"Was that Peter's tape?" he asked his daughter. "What was going on down here?"

"Nothing was going on." Peter spoke a little painfully. "She was just – thanking me and I tripped, that's all."

"Oh boy! Mary Ann," Michael smiled. "Your thanks packs a hefty punch!" Everybody grinned weakly.

"What's going on?" Robert appeared in the doorway clutching his bag of presents.

"Come on then," Michael said after belated Happy Christmases all round. "As we're all up, let's open our presents now. Jane, you fetch ours and I'll turn on the heating. It's freezing in here – there's a terrible fog outside."

In the happiness of opening their presents, letting the room fill up with brightly coloured paper and glittering ribbon, no one really noticed when Mary Ann began to watch her Christmas video again. She turned it on very low and crouched in front of it, becoming lost to everything else.

Later, when she played it again after breakfast, Michael watched the opening titles. The Winter King was seen inviting his viewers into his palace cut deep into the heart of a mountain and lit with dozens of flaming torches. Here he would entertain his "guests" with marvellous stories.

"Seems to me that hoary old man is a new version of the Lord of Misrule," he said to Jane, who was gathering up some of the Christmas debris.

"Oh, him!" remarked Robert. "Got you!" he said to Peter. The boys were playing his new board game.

"The telly puts me off," Peter complained without too much irritation. "It's that stupid old codger with the mistle-toe on his head."

"The Lord of Misrule," repeated Jane thoughtfully, paus-ing to look. "The pauper who is made king for the day. He looks a bit like it. He's the one who can do what he pleases during his reign and things can get turned upside down."

"The Lord of Disruption indeed," Michael agreed, stoop-ing to put an arm round his intent, watching daughter. "I wouldn't have him around at Christmas myself."

On the screen the Winter King was introducing his first story for the second time that day. He took a big gulp from his goblet, wiped his mouth on the back of his hand and said,

"'Bye now, girls and boys! I'll be seeing you," and his pointing finger came straight at them.

"Don't like the look in his eye," added Michael.

But Mary Ann only sighed with anticipation, impatient for the new story to begin. Michael stroked her smooth hair. She turned to him and rubbed her cheek against his rough jumper. Her father felt an acute pang of loss for the little daughter he could only see at prescribed times. He was very fond of Jane's boys, of course he was, but it was hard sometimes. . . . He left the sitting room abruptly and went to see to the boiler. The house was still feeling cold.

Everyone heard the crash this time. Michael had lost his footing on the old, rather rickety cellar steps and tumbled helplessly to the bottom. Robert reached him first.

"I think he's OK, Mum," he called up to the little group standing in the doorway at the top of the steps.

"I'm quite all right. Don't fuss, Jane." Michael spoke testily although Jane hadn't said anything at all. "Give us a hand up, Robert. My ankle's twisted."

With Robert's help he limped painfully up the steps and lowered himself into a sitting room chair. Jane took off his shoe and rolled down his sock.

"Ice pack," she said. "Robert, get a towel and Peter, fetch a rug. I'll get the ice. What's the matter with my family today?"

Ice pack in place, Jane tucked the rug round his knees. "Don't you dare move," she told him. "We'll all have lunch in here – somehow. You stay put."

"Have a feel of my bump," Peter said kindly. "It's enormous. It'll make you feel better!"

Mary Ann, having seen that her father was not seriously hurt, had returned to her place in front of the video.

"I'll be seeing you!" The Winter King was saying again.

"He's beginning to get on my nerves," thought Peter as the now familiar shiver began its journey up his back. "And Mary Ann is really odd, the way she just watches and watches."

The family busied themselves with arranging lunch in the sitting room. They all felt a bit light-headed, as people do when their plans have gone very wrong but not quite as badly wrong as they might have done.

It was a splendid lunch with all the trimmings, but sitting hunched up over their plates on their knees, or bending over the low coffee tables and having to rush out to get everything from the kitchen, spoilt its usual pleasure. They did their best to appreciate Jane's cooking and by the time they were ready for the pudding things were going reasonably well.

Mary Ann had turned down the sound on the TV but the pictures continued to tell the stories, and sitting next to it she watched them out of the corner of her eyes. Peter sat firmly with his back to the set, doing all he could to resist the temptation to look at the Winter King. Each time he heard the words "I'll be seeing you," he couldn't stop his thoughts spinning back to the young man he had met in the street: the strange young man with icy blue eyes – exactly like the Winter King's blue eyes – who had read his thoughts so clearly.

"Mary Ann, come and help me turn out the pudding." Jane wanted to include her. "We have to warm the brandy before we can light it, so we'll need some matches."

Mary Ann rose obediently. Peter could see she didn't want to leave the TV. He found himself watching her a lot. He wasn't sure why exactly, but he felt he needed to keep her within sight in case she . . . what? He didn't know.

It was this feeling that made him leave the sitting room and go to the kitchen door to watch the ceremony of the pudding.

Jane lifted the pudding basin out of the boiling water and carried it carefully to the draining board. Mary Ann brought the pudding plate and watched as the basin was up-ended over it and given a good shake. With a gentle sigh the pudding left the basin and landed whole and complete in the centre of the plate. Jane shook on some sugar and Mary Ann stuck in the small sprig of holly they had saved for this moment.

Peter clapped. "Well done, Mum!" His feeling of relief surprised him.

Mary Ann echoed, "Well done! It's perfect – clever you!" and she hugged her round the waist. Jane glowed. She had hoped that Mary Ann would have a good time with them and she was touched by her spontaneous warmth.

Some warning bell in Peter's head began to ring but he still couldn't make the connection. He watched his mother turn to carry out the pudding. "Get the matches, Peter," she said happily. Then the plate broke.

The pudding, hot and steaming, plunged down and lay in large dollops over both her feet.

Jane dropped the two pieces of plate and screamed with pain as the scalding pudding began to burn through her stockings.

"Get it off me!" she shouted, reaching for the top of her tights and trying to drag them off. Peter struggled awkwardly to help her. Mary Ann ran into the sitting room, shocked and frightened. Michael, wrapped in his rug, struggled to rise and Robert dashed into the kitchen to stand helplessly by while his mother, sobbing with pain, finally rid herself of stockings and pudding.

"Water!" she cried, turning to the taps and running cold water into the washing-up basin.

"Jane! What on earth have you done?" Michael had got to the kitchen and was clinging onto the door frame.

Robert helped his mother to a chair and brought the basin so that she could gingerly sink her burning scarlet feet into its cooling depths.

"The plate must have had a crack and I didn't see it," she said as she waited for the water to ease the pain a little. "It just broke. Honestly, Michael," she laughed a little shakily, "just look at us both!"

Her husband sank down onto a kitchen chair. He smiled ruefully. "And Peter, don't forget – three down and two to go." He sighed as he reached for her hand to give it a squeeze.

Robert scraped the last pieces of pudding into the bin and put the kettle on.

"Hot sweet tea all round," he said.

"I don't believe it!" thought Peter. "Mary Ann is at that video again." He went to look. There she was, crouched over as he had first seen her that morning, staring at the screen. Peter's sense of unease gripped him as he watched her. The Winter King brought yet another story to a close.

"If I hear those words again I'll do something really violent," he muttered as the beastly shiver started its journey up his backbone. The violence in his mind seemed to join the violence that had injured his parents and hurt himself and centre in the crouching, gentle figure of his step-sister. He shoved the picture of the Winter King's blue eyes away from him. "I'm going potty or I'll wake up soon," he thought frantically. "It's still bitterly cold in here. No wonder I'm shivering. What's the matter with the boiler? What's the matter with everything?"

Jane's feet were gently dried and brushed with some soothing powder from the medicine cupboard. They were slightly swollen and small blisters had begun to form. She reassured everyone that if they were worse in the morning she would go to Casualty. She'd wait and see.

Pudding wasn't mentioned again, but dates and nuts were circulated as the family continued their Christmas Day. They pulled their crackers and tried to have fun, but somehow the jokes inside seemed feebler than usual and no one kept their paper hats on very long. It became obvious that the best thing they could do was to settle down as comfortably as possible and watch the afternoon film on TV.

Only Mary Ann wasn't happy. That would mean she couldn't get to the end of her Winter King stories. There seemed to be an endless supply – or perhaps she just kept rewinding the tape. No one was quite sure.

Peter's patience was beginning to fray. The bump on his head was still sore and he had a slight headache. He felt he would do anything to get that video out of the room.

"If the Lord of Misrule brings disruption like Michael says, then the Winter King seems to be top of the league!" he thought. His thoughts rushed on. "And Mary Ann's in there with him too." But how could she be? There wasn't any evidence that she had anything to do with his family's accidents. In fact she was always being loving just before . . . "just before . . ." Peter tried to remember. "She kissed me, and I fell over. She was loving to Michael before he fell down the cellar steps. And she hugged Mum before— but that's stupid! Or is it?"

"Oh, for goodness' sake, let her take the video machine upstairs to my room," he heard himself saying. "She can watch all she wants there."

A feeling of relief spread through the family. Robert got up. "I'll fix it for her," he said promptly. "Come on, Mary Ann, we'll get the darned thing going for you up there."

"Robert!" Peter almost shouted.

Robert stopped in his tracks and Peter faltered. How could he say "Be careful of Mary Ann. Don't let her get too close, especially if she's grateful"? They'd think he'd flipped. He wasn't sure he hadn't.

"Oh, just don't, I mean . . . oh, nothing really . . ."

"Bump on the head's finished him off." Robert raised a scathing eyebrow and followed Mary Ann's impatient back view out of the room.

214

Peter's feeling of anxiety threatened to overpower him. "It's far worse if I can't see her," he thought as he waited in agony for his brother to return.

Robert came back just as the film was starting, wrapping one of his hands in a handkerchief. It was bleeding.

"Robert!" Jane looked at his hand in disbelief.

"Did she kiss you?" Peter blurted out.

"What?"

"For fixing her video. Did she thank you?"

"What have you done to your hand?" his mother demanded.

"I just cut it. All right?" Robert was irritated by the questions. "And no, she didn't kiss me. All right?"

"But she hugged you?"

Robert looked at Peter, his irritation mounting.

"I don't believe this!" Michael's voice cut across Robert's reply. "Now the television's gone on the blink!"

It was. The images rolled in streaky lines across the screen, their brilliance pulsing. Then, with a cross between a cough and a hiccup, it went black.

It was the last straw. Robert, his exasperation over-flowing, turned on his step-father. "It's a rotten set. It's come out of the ark. I'm going to Roger's. At least I know his set will work – it's not a hundred years old!" He stormed out of the room.

Peter got up and turned off the dead set; he was the only mobile one left, apart from Mary Ann. Now he was certain – well, as certain as anyone could be – that contact with Mary Ann triggered off the family's accidents. He knew that the video was also part of it, but was at a loss to understand how.

Jane's face was white and miserable, Michael's not much better. How could he say, "It's all happened because of Mary Ann"? Or worse, how could he say "Mum, Michael, it's all my fault. It's all happening because I was too mean to spend my money on a decent present"? Impossible.

Peter made up his mind. Mary Ann, and the video, would be gone tomorrow. He would just have to make sure nothing else happened before then – if he could.

So they tried to carry on what was left of their Christmas, but it was uphill work. The house got so cold, even though the boiler was going full blast, that they ended up wrapped in blankets as they listened to tapes and played Scrabble in a half-hearted way.

Robert returned in time to eat a simple supper. Mary Ann was content to eat hers on a tray, glued to Peter's old TV. She only came down to say good night when Robert was sent to tell her it was time to get ready for bed.

She came into the room in a brisk, matter-of-fact sort of way. Peter thought she would just say good night and go – he wasn't prepared for the way she advanced on Jane and Michael, throwing her arms round each one and kissing them.

"Thank you so much for a lovely Christmas!" she said. "It's been the best Christmas ever!"

Peter looked on in dismay. How could she say that? He felt powerless even to get up from his chair, frozen with horror. He hadn't stopped her. He hadn't even been able to try!

Then she went over to where Robert sat slumped in his chair, struggling with the bumper crossword.

"Good night, Robert," she said.

Peter tried to speak. His words wouldn't get going – they seemed to be stuck firmly in his throat. He just gurgled.

Robert, lost in a complicated anagram, barely looked up.

"'Night," was all he said.

Then Mary Ann turned to face Peter. Panic rose in him like a tidal wave.

"Got to go!" he yelped, jerking himself out of his chair and nearly knocking her over. "Toilet!" he shouted as he slammed the door. His heart was pounding. She had kissed his parents and he hadn't done a thing to stop her. Now what would happen?

Everyone else went to bed just after ten o'clock, clutching hot water bottles. As he cleaned his teeth Peter could see that icicles were actually forming on the inside of the bathroom window. They reminded him of the Winter King's crown on the cover of the video. "He's taking over," he thought, and shuddered.

Jane and Michael managed to undress as best they could, given their injuries. They were both very tired. As they eased themselves under the duvet, Jane said,

"I ought to go and see if Mary Ann has settled down."

"She's probably still stuck in front of that wretched video." Michael winced as he caught his foot. "I doubt if we could stop her."

"Oh well, maybe it's the best thing to let her be tonight. We don't want a fuss and she's only got until tomorrow."

The boys undressed silently. Neither of them had anything to say about the disastrous day. Robert got into bed, plugged into his walkman and opened a book.

"How can he do both at the same time?" wondered Peter, snuggling down into his sleeping bag and trying to get his feet warm. He couldn't read. He could only lie tense and rigid with a huge cold lump in his stomach and anxiety racing through his mind.

He felt scared and he felt guilty. The words "I'll be seeing you" rang through his aching head. He didn't know if Mary Ann knew what was happening, he didn't think she did. None of it really made any sense. The piercing eyes of the strange young man and the bearded Winter King swam in his brain. They bored into him. He couldn't get away. Both faces seemed to melt into one as they looked at him. He felt utterly helpless.

He could hear the sounds of the tape coming through the bedroom wall – she was still at it. Why wouldn't she stop?

An hour later his tired eyes shut and he slept. . . .

Two hours later the television set in the sitting room began to smoulder.

The fire started in the plug and soon the wire flared up. Then the curtains, falling in front of the plug, caught alight and the paper streamers blazed.

Peter woke up at the sound of the curtain pole falling. He sat bolt upright, wide awake at once. His ragged senses shouted, trouble!

Wriggling quickly out of bed he paused at the top of the stairs, terrified. Smoke was billowing from the sitting room door.

He flung his parents' bedroom door open with a crash. "Fire!" he shouted. "Quick! Wake up!"

Robert came on to the landing. "My God!" he whispered. He rushed into his parents' room, knowing they would need his help to move fast.

Peter burst into Mary Ann's room and stopped short.

The TV was on and she was crouching close to it as if her very life depended on the flickering screen.

Horrified, Peter grabbed her by the shoulders and yanked her away just as the familiar words of the Winter King were forming.

Mary Ann's screams blotted them out. She continued screaming as Peter dragged her down the stairs and out into the still foggy night where Jane and Michael fought to quieten her. She would not stop.

"It's not the fire," Peter knew. "She's not screaming because of the fire." He thought of the tape continuing to play in the deserted house and he was filled with terror.

Standing in a huddle on the front lawn, the dazed family watched the firemen get the fire under control. Neighbours clustered round, lending blankets, getting hot drinks and giving them refuge for the night. Never, never had there been a Christmas Day like that one.

Boxing Day morning dawned frosty and bright, not a vestige of fog anywhere. Peter and his family entered their troubled home as soon as they could. Upstairs was almost untouched, but downstairs – what a mess!

"I've sent for Joanna," Michael said. "We'd better get Mary Ann's things together."

"I can do it." Mary Ann was standing behind them.

"You made me jump," said Jane. "I thought you were still having breakfast." But she was grateful not to be doing too much walking up and down.

Peter watched Mary Ann's slight form slip upstairs. "She's come back for the tape," he thought. "Why didn't I throw it away when I could?"

He made a dash for the stairs and got to his bedroom door just as Mary Ann removed the tape. The firemen had stopped the Winter King in full flood.

Mary Ann smiled at him. "I couldn't leave your present, could I? It was the best."

As he looked at her, Peter knew then that she could read his thoughts like a book. Unable to speak, he flattened himself against the door and let her pass. There was nothing he could do.

Later, when Joanna had come for Mary Ann and they were gathered to see her off, Peter thought, "At least that's the last we'll see of her and the Winter King. They're not going to be in our house any more . . ." and then he felt miserable and guilty for thinking it. Should he try to warn Joanna? He knew he couldn't.

Mary Ann said subdued goodbyes to everyone as they stood in their ruined front garden. Then, before getting into her mother's car, she turned to say something to Peter. He stepped back involuntarily, alarm flooding him.

"Oh, don't worry, Peter," she said, looking straight at him, "I'm not going to kiss you, but—" and she smiled, "I'll be seeing you!"

Peter gasped. He put out a hand to steady himself. Mary Ann's eyes, not quite anything before, were now a piercing, icy blue!

THE HIGHWAYMAN'S LAST RIDE

Malcolm Rose

"I want to speak to Jane."

Emma hesitated before replying, "She's not here right now."

Jane's father grunted. "What do you mean? She's supposed to be with you."

Jane often told her dad that she was visiting Emma when in fact she was going to her boyfriend's place.

"I mean, she's just popped out." Emma did not normally lie and she found it difficult. With Jane's dad on the telephone, though, she was prepared to make an exception. It seemed entirely justified to deceive a man like him. The deception was more than counterbalanced by the act of kindness towards Jane. But Emma did wish that Jane had forewarned her about seeing Rick.

"Popped out? Has she indeed?"

"Yes. To the shop. I'll give her a message if you like, when she gets back – any time now."

"You do that."

"What's the message, then?" Emma asked.

"Tell her to come home. Right now. Her mum needs her."

Before Emma could reply, he rang off. She spoke into the purring receiver: "Yes, certainly I'll be happy to deliver your message, Mr Woodward."

She dialled and waited some time for a response. "Hello, Rick," she said, "It's Emma here. Can I speak to Jane?"

Immediately Rick began his familiar banter. "How do you know she's here?"

"Just a hunch," Emma answered.

"Okay, Sherlock. I'll get her."

There was another delay before Jane came on the line. "Hi. What's up?" she said.

"Your time, I'm afraid. I've just had your dad on the line."

"Ah."

"Yes. Ah."

"Did he realise I wasn't with you?"

"I don't know. I'd have performed better if you'd warned me. I told him you'd nipped out to the shops."

"Sorry, Emma. It slipped my mind. Thanks, anyway," Jane said. "I just have to hope he didn't cotton on about Rick. Otherwise, we're for it."

It wasn't the first time that Jane's dad had objected to a boyfriend. None of them seemed to be good enough for his Jane. Rick, in particular, wasn't up to scratch. It was a pity, Emma thought, because there was something special between Jane and Rick. No sensible father would disapprove of Rick. He did have one black mark – a case of shoplifting – but he was kind and dependable. Certainly respectable enough to take home to the old folks. Not to Jane's dad, though. Boyfriends were taboo.

"What did Dad want?" Jane continued.

"He wants you home. Pronto. Said your mum needs you."

"Poor Mum. Hope she's all right. Heaven help us if he's found out . . . Oh, never mind. You know what it means, don't you?"

"No."

"It means he's beaten her up. A rage or a binge, no doubt. Afterwards, he never knows what to do. Pathetic. Probably drunk. That's why he hates me to go out. I'd better go back and sort it out."

"Okay," Emma replied. "But before you go, Jane, don't

use me as alibi till after Christmas. Remember Dad's taking me on a Christmas break. We're about to leave. Tomorrow and Christmas Day in Wetherby. Saves him having to cook on the big day."

"Oh, yeah. Sorry, Emma. You did tell me – ages ago. It'd gone completely out of my mind. Too many other things to worry about. You know – problems at home and all. Anyway, where did you say you were staying?" she asked. "Not camping, I hope!"

"At this time of year? No chance. A hotel. A hotel with a secret, Dad says. Won't tell me what the secret is."

"Sounds interesting."

"Sounds cringy."

"Oh, go and enjoy it. You're lucky. You wouldn't get my dad to take us anywhere – or give us anything but the nastiest of surprises."

Jane had been preoccupied with her own problems but there was another reason why she'd forgotten about the trip. Emma had hardly mentioned it on purpose. She knew that Jane envied her easy relationship with her father and to dwell on their Christmas treat would have rubbed salt in her friend's wounds.

"I'm sorry, Jane," Emma said. "I wish your dad wasn't so . . . you know. Anyway, I'll call you from the hotel, Christmas morning. Sneak it onto Dad's bill. He won't notice. I'll catch up on how things went then. Okay?"

"Sure. I'd better get going."

"All the best. Take care."

As soon as Emma hung up, her father shouted down from his bedroom, "Who was that?"

"Mr Woodward. Jane's dad."

"Oh, him." Her father's tone was derogatory. "Don't cross paths with him, Emma, if you don't have to."

Emma had introduced her dad to Jane's family at some school function, a while ago. He mixed well with them but soon learned that polite exchanges with Mr Woodward were almost impossible.

Coming down the stairs with his suitcase in his hand, he queried, "What did he want?"

"Jane."

"Don't tell me. Jane's at . . . er . . ."

"Yes. Rick's place."

Her dad shook his head. "As I said, Emma, be careful."

"Yes, I know. But I have to protect her. You know what he'll do if he finds out about Rick?" Emma asked sadly.

"Give her several clips around the ear, minimum, I expect," he replied. "Horrible bloke. I'll never understand why Jane's mother married him. Still," he added, "I'm in no position to talk."

Emma smiled at him weakly. Changing the subject, she commented, "Big case for a weekend. Hope you've packed my present – and your chequebook."

"At least I'm further ahead than you, my girl," he replied. "Go on. Get cracking. Finish off your packing while I check we're all locked up, ready for the off."

The weather forecasters had poured cold water on the chances of snow at Christmas. Mornings were misty and nights cold and crisp. Freezing fog was forecast. Hardly a greetings-card Christmas.

King's Lynn behind them, Emma and her father headed north-west. "Easy drive," her dad said. "Should be there just before dark. Even I can't get lost when there's only two roads: the A17 and then the A1 itself. The Great North Road. Haunt of many a highwayman. And we're headed to a hotel called The Highwayman."

"What's it like, this place?" Emma asked.

"I don't know. Converted old manor house, I'm told."

"With a secret."

"Of course."

"You're not letting on yet, then?"

Her dad was determined to maintain the mystery for as

long as possible. "Certainly not," he replied with a smile. "Wait and see."

"Long wait, isn't it? Quite a long drive."

"Not too bad. But I don't need a navigator, so you can get some shut-eye if you like." He glanced at her with an impish grin and added, "You might need it."

Emma looked at him quizzically. "Why?"

"Late nights. That sort of thing."

"Oh?"

"All part of the surprise."

The Highwayman Hotel was set apart from the town in its own grounds, which bounded open countryside. Constructed around an old cobbled courtyard with stables on two sides, the building was plain and grim. The weathered stone walls leaned in all the wrong directions. Its six chimney stacks were tall enough to give Santa Claus vertigo. Ivy clung tenaciously to one side. The house looked as if it would be full of secret passages and huge, dismal oil paintings. It would have a locked room where a despicable crime had once been committed. At night everything would creak eerily and a whimper emanate from the locked room. Or maybe the owner would be a crazed, satanic killer.

In fact, the interior was bright rather than dingy, hung

with stark modern photographs, and their host greeted them cordially. He insisted that they should call him Mike. "We're not a big hotel," he told them. "We pride ourselves on a family atmosphere. No formalities here. Mike will do for me."

After getting them to sign the register, Mike handed a leaflet to her dad. "This," he said, "tells you all about tomorrow's—"

"Yes," her dad interrupted. "Thanks." He pocketed the notice while he explained, "I want it to be a surprise for Emma."

Mike turned to Emma and said, "What a cruel dad you've got. Still, I can't spill the beans. Never upset the guest wielding the chequebook. That's my motto." Beaming, Mike addressed her dad again. "Keeping it a secret shouldn't be too difficult. At Christmas, we don't need to shout about our claim to fame. We could fill the hotel three times over without a murmur about . . . you know."

Emma's room overlooked the courtyard and, in the distance, the Yorkshire Dales. For a while she took in the view, muttering to herself, "Mmm. Real hills for a change."

Standing by the window and averting her eyes from a string of pylons, she could believe that time had sloughed off a couple of centuries. Without roads in view, she could imagine an older, unhurried world. A world where mothers did not run away with other men and fathers did not beat their daughters. Really, she knew that desertion and cruelty were not confined to the modern world – to her and Jane – but they seemed more remote as she gazed across the peaceful countryside. She looked up at the sky and said, "Soon be dark."

Inside, the shell of her room was old and authentic, with an ornate ceiling and quaint leaded windows. The furniture, though, was new and functional. If she had hoped for a four-poster bed, she would have been disappointed. She twirled around and smiled anyway. "Nice. Small but comfortable," she murmured happily. "Good old Dad!"

Emma looked around the rest of the tables and felt the discomfort that always accompanied such occasions. All the other diners were couples or complete families. Somehow, it seemed inappropriate to be having a candle-lit dinner with just a father. The romance of it all was wasted. She wondered if any of the other guests were looking askance at them. Her mind quickly turned to Jane. Emma wouldn't really want to sacrifice Christmas away with her dad, but she would gladly have given their places at the dinner table to Jane and Rick. They deserved some real romance instead of the snatched and sordid trysts that cheapened their relationship.

"Emma?" Her dad brought her back down to earth.

"Yes?"

"Enjoying it?"

"Mmm. Very good," she replied.

"I've been meaning to . . . er . . . ask you something."

"What's that?" she prompted.

"I don't know. I feel . . . well . . . as if I can't offer you everything a girl should have."

"How do you mean?"

He took a gulp of wine. "What I mean is . . . do you miss having a mother?"

Emma smiled sympathetically at her dad. "You're enough for me. In fact, I can hardly cope with one parent. How would I manage with two?"

He returned her smile but responded insistently, "Really, though."

"If I'd had a good mum, I'd miss her, no doubt. But I don't miss her."

"Can you remember her at all? Good *or* bad," he asked.

"Not really. I was too young."

"I suppose so," he replied. "She wasn't . . . necessarily a bad mother – or wife, you know. She just wasn't ready to commit herself to a family."

"I don't have to remember her to know that I'd rather be with you."

"How come?"

232

"I wouldn't want to be with a mother who can't even be bothered to send me a Christmas card." Despite herself, Emma felt tears in her eyes.

Her father put down his fork and squeezed her hand. "I know."

She sniffed and wiped her eyes. "It's silly. No point in getting upset or angry." She looked around the room, hoping that no one had witnessed her moment of weakness.

"Sometimes it's better to call it a day, you know – to end an unhappy relationship. Look what happens when people cling to a hopeless one."

"You mean Jane's family?"

Her dad nodded. "If you can call it a family when it's held together by threats."

"I see what you mean," she said. "We should feel privileged compared to that."

"I still think you'd prefer to have a mum, though. It'd be better for you."

Emma shrugged and tried to cheer them up. "You're not about to spring another surprise on me, are you? A mother for Christmas?"

He hesitated then shook his head. "No. I was . . . just thinking."

"Do *you* ever think of Mum?" Emma asked him.

He considered for a moment and answered, "No. Not

really. I'm sure she's happier wherever she is. I'm sure we're all better off the way it is. And I don't think I bear a grudge. I've got too many other things on my mind to worry about what happened ages ago."

"Quite right," Emma told him, like a matron.

"Anyway, this meal's not getting the attention it deserves, is it?"

"Mmm. And no washing up after. Makes it taste even better!"

They tucked in.

On the morning of Christmas Eve, the promised fog arrived. After a breakfast that was substantial enough to pass as a lunch, Emma and her father drove cautiously through the mist to take a look at Harrogate, but the clutter of last-minute shoppers soon forced them away. By then much of the fog had cleared and so they went hiking in the Dales. In the more desolate spots, they could imagine being the only people alive. The residual haze added mystery rather than danger. They walked and talked happily until dusk.

After dinner that night, they watched a film on the television in the lounge. It was nearly midnight when it finished and Emma declared that she was going to her room. "I'll come up with you," her dad said.

"Oh. Okay," she replied. "But I don't need putting to bed these days, you know."

Even at that time of night, the foyer buzzed with guests. Perhaps, Emma thought, they were on their way to Midnight Mass. That would explain why they were all wearing coats.

As Emma climbed the stairs, her dad said, "Are you sure you're ready for bed?"

"What do you mean?" She looked at her watch. "Nearly Christmas Day, you know. I'm tired after all that walking."

They entered her bedroom and her dad continued, "You're on your holidays. Everyone stops up late on their hols."

Emma went over to the window to draw the curtains but saw something outside that caught her eye. She stood with her hands on the curtains but did not pull them together. "There's something strange outside, Dad," she said, frowning.

In the courtyard, there were several groups of lights, some still, some moving about. She jumped a little as her dad came up behind her. "What's going on?" she asked.

Clearly in the know, he answered playfully, "I wonder!"

"Stop teasing!" she cried.

"Come on." He took her arm and propelled her towards the door. "It's beginning. Grab your coat. It'll be freezing out there."

"It's the surprise! The secret!"

He smiled broadly. "Yes. The secret's out. The hotel's

haunted! Ghosts wave mysterious lights about in the yard at midnight on Christmas Eve."

"They're no ghosts," Emma protested, but followed her dad anyway.

"No," he replied. "But it *is* a haunted hotel." He reached around the door of his own room and grabbed his coat. "And what you saw was the ghost train."

"What?"

"Well, the ghost tour, anyway. They take the punters on a midnight tour of the ghosts' favourite haunts." He stopped at the top of the stairs and encouraged her. "Come on. Coat on. It'll be fun."

"Oh, all right." She followed him down the stairs and into the hall where they were given "candles", battery operated to defeat the wind.

Out in the cobbled courtyard, they joined the other guests, all holding their torches aloft. To distinguish himself, Mike, who was acting as their guide, held a spooky green light.

"Okay," he called. "I think we're all here. Let the tour begin! Follow me."

He led them across the yard to the stables, and then stopped. "Gather round," he called. When all the guests were assembled he lowered his voice and continued. "Here in the stables a girl can sometimes be heard sobbing pitifully.

Two hundred years ago Tess, the master's daughter, used to have secret meetings here with her lover, Matthew the highwayman. Handsome enough to attract any woman, Matty was, but he was loyal only to Tess, and each month he would slip into this yard to see her. It's still the same place. From 1792 to today, it hasn't changed a bit. Inside this stable, out of view of everyone, they carried on their affair. That is, until one night when they were overheard. Just here by the stable door, you can imagine Jim, the stable lad, crouching and listening. A calamity for Tess and Matty because Jim was faithful to the squire. As soon as Matty had ridden away over the moor, Jim ran to the master and told his tale. The squire's daughter cavorting with a highwayman! When he heard, the master flew into a rage. Poor Tess. He beat her till she bled and pleaded for mercy."

"Has anyone actually *seen* her?" some eager guest enquired, perhaps hoping that fresh blood might drip onto the cobbles.

"No. Nothing's been seen," Mike answered solemnly. "There's just her sobbing."

Emma shivered. Their guide, the misty night and the pretend candles were creating an eerie atmosphere that made her feel colder than she already was. There was something about the story, though, that engaged her. Something about Tess and Matty. Their plight was familiar.

Her father nudged her and whispered, "Good, eh?"

"Mmm."

"The squire wasted no time," the manager continued in his well-practiced whisper. "He forced Tess to marry the old and lecherous Lord Metford. A speedy arrangement and a profitable marriage, but Tess loathed him. Imagine," he went on, "the wedding party riding back from the church, passing through the gate over there and clattering over these same cobbles up to the door of the old house. Old Metford grinning and slavering. Tess dreading the rest of her life – life without her beloved Matty." He paused for their imaginations to catch up with him. "Now we go into a part of the house that hasn't been touched for two hundred years, to see the room in which Tess was prepared for her fearful wedding night."

They traipsed inside and up two flights of dimly-lit stairs. The glow from their torches danced on the walls and ceiling as they climbed. The bride's room was musty and the old oak panelling made it dingy. Hardly a joyous place.

"Turn off your torches," Mike ordered quietly. He sat in the high-backed chair before a large mirror with an elaborate wooden frame. The green light from his torch reflected back into the room. "This," he proclaimed, "is where the lovely Tess sat while her maids arranged her hair and nightgown before Lord Metford's arrival." He sighed. "Tess must have been thinking of her dashing young man, not her appearance. She shooed away the maids to wait in solitude and grief." The green glow rose as Mike left the chair and tiptoed over to the bed. He perched on its edge. "It's here," he said respectfully, as if Tess herself could hear him, "that she must have made up her mind. Life without her Matty was not worth living. She could not bear the thought of Lord Metford. She could not allow herself to be despoiled by him." He looked up momentarily at his entranced audience. "She rose when she heard his knock at the door." Mike stamped his foot on the floor, making them all jump with shock. Then their guide stood up and, in a high-pitched voice, cried, "I will not yield! I would rather die!" Suddenly he dashed across the room, yelling, "Matty!"

He may not have turned out to be a crazed serial killer but he was certainly a little crazy. He ran into the curtains on the opposite side of the room and flung them open. "This, ladies and gentlemen," he announced, "is where Tess threw herself out of the window!"

Several of the guests gasped.

Mike's voice became a whisper again. "Yes. The day that Tess married was also the day that she died." He turned to his guests. "We're two floors up. As she intended, the fall killed her. But at least she remained untainted by the old man." He drew together the heavy curtains, then said, "It's

239

lights-on time. We'll go down below to see the spot where she died."

Emma's host had cast a web and the guests had become enmeshed in it one by one. They knew it was a show but it did not seem like a sham. In her turn, Emma too was captivated.

Mike led the guests back outside where the air was colder still. Their breath became visible by the light of their torches. He guided them along the path that followed the contours of the house until they reached the point directly below the window of the bride's room. Pointing to the ground, he said, "Here we are. Do you notice anything? Lower your torches."

They peered at the ground earnestly, as if someone had dropped a twenty-pound note. No one failed to look down. Mike had engrossed and convinced them all.

"Yes!" someone called. "I see it."

"What?" another guest queried.

"Everywhere there's grass but not here. The earth's black."

"That's right," Mike confirmed. "For years, nothing's grown on the spot where she died. Absolutely nothing."

Of course, he could have poured weedkiller on the patch yesterday, but none of the visitors believed that he had.

"Is that the end?" Emma asked her dad.

She blushed when she realized that even a whisper carried far in a quiet night. "No," the manager replied. "Not at all. The final act, the final horror, happened over there." He pointed to an old oak tree. "You see, Lord Metford and Tess's father hatched a plot with the local sheriff. They knew that when the highwayman heard of Tess's fate he'd come for them. And they were right."

He beckoned them to walk behind him to the oak beside a track. As they strolled across the lawn, frozen leaves crunched underfoot. The bark of the tree and the grass beneath had grown crystals of ice like old men's whiskers. Between the branches hung tangles of string that had once been translucent cobwebs. In the faint light, the track was a pale ribbon across the dark moor.

Mike pointed to the west. "That's where he came from – the old drove road from Grassington in the Dales. He knew it well because in Wetherby it linked with the original Great North Road where he conducted much of his business. Christmas Day, it was, in the year 1792, when Matty rode furiously over the moor, a sword in his hand. He was crying. Crying aloud for his Tess, for revenge. A cry of anger and dismay." He paused for dramatic effect. "The sheriff had never been able to catch him before. He was too cunning for that. But this was different. This time the sheriff had fifty paid men crouching either side of the road. The wind howled through the trees as Matty rode into the trap. What could one do against fifty mercenaries?" Another theatrical pause. "He knew that it was a trap, of course. Knew that he was riding to his death. But he was a man of honour, and utterly devoted to Tess. What was his life without her?" Mike shrugged, signifying pointlessness.

"He rode along here, brandishing his sword. As the mercenaries jumped out, Matty slashed at them, this way and that. But he was hopelessly outnumbered. As Lord Metford, the sheriff and the squire looked on and laughed cruelly, Matty was dragged from his horse, just here." He shuffled a little to stand in the exact place beside the tree. "They bound him, flung the rope over that bough there – the thick black one – and hanged him right here." He held high his green light. "His last roar was full of hatred and anguish. He howled like the wind. And when he died, the wind died too."

Mike lowered his voice and his light. "The mercenaries crept away in the quiet night like thieves, leaving a good man hanging here for the birds." He sighed again. "Even the birds must have flown away in guilt because, from that day to this, no bird has ever been seen to perch on this tree. Now, some say that on Christmas Day, when the wind howls through the trees, you can see Matty the highwayman riding across the moor in anguish and hear his dreadful scream on the wind. So you see," he concluded, addressing Emma directly, "it's still not over. Not really. Keep your eyes peeled tomorrow – or later today, I should say. It's two hundred years exactly. Matty will ride once more."

Emma shivered. Mike's final words had stung her. "It's still not over," she said to herself. "Not really. Matty will ride once more." She didn't know why, but she could not shake the words out of her head.

Cold but exhilarated, the residents made their way across the grounds, over the cobbles and back into the hotel. In the foyer, they were provided with a hot drink before they dispersed to their rooms.

"There you are," Emma's dad said to her. "A hotel with a difference." He looked into her face and asked, "Are you all right?"

"Yes," she fibbed. "Just frozen and tired, I guess."

"Enjoyed it, though?"

"Mmm. As you said – different!"

But that night, as she lay awake in her warm bed, Mike's words repeated endlessly inside her head like the unwelcome refrain of a catchy song. "*It's not over yet . . . Full of hatred and anguish is his roar . . . Christmas Day, the highwayman will ride once more.*"

* * *

Before she sat down at the breakfast table, Emma kissed her dad. "Thanks, Dad!" she said.

"You found it, then?"

"Yes. Lovely dress. I'll wear it later. See what you think."

"It's not me that counts – I think you always look great. Except that you look worn out this morning. Up too late or nightmares?"

"Neither really," she replied. She sat down heavily. "Just couldn't sleep. Some of the things Mike said last night. I can't help applying them to . . . Oh, I don't know. Forget it."

Her dad looked concerned. "I'm sorry if my little surprise upset you. It wasn't supposed to. Let's eat breakfast. See if it'll put the colour back in your cheeks."

"Okay." Emma did not feel able to explain her uneasiness. Her thoughts were too jumbled. Besides, irrational fears cannot be rationalized.

"Last night," her dad said, still trying to reassure her, "was just harmless fun, you know. Standard folklore. Sung in a million folk songs. Mike's embroidered the story a bit, no doubt, for dramatic effect."

Emma wanted to believe him but her intuition told her otherwise. Even so, to make her dad feel better, she nodded and murmured, "Yes."

"Besides," he added, "no self-respecting highwayman

would ride out in this." He jerked his head towards the window. The fog was much thicker and more obstinate than Christmas Eve's. "A whole regiment could ride past the hotel this morning and we wouldn't see a thing. Let's hope it clears this evening for the drive home."

"Dad," Emma asked, "Do you mind if I call Jane? There's a phone in my room."

"Sure," he answered. "But try to finish before lunch."

"Thanks."

Emma asked the receptionist to put her through to Jane's King's Lynn number. It rang a good few times before someone answered, "Hello?"

Emma groaned inwardly. It was Mr Woodward's voice. "Can I speak to Jane, please?"

"What for?"

"It's Emma here. I just want to wish her a happy Christmas."

Mr Woodward cackled, just as Emma imagined that the squire would have done as Matty was hanged. Her spine tingled as he went on, "Happy! It's all right for some. Away enjoying themselves. Playing Happy Families." He snorted. "I'll get her for you."

"Jane!" Emma breathed. "How is it?"

"Well . . . er . . . I don't know, Emma. It's a bit difficult to say."

"Why? What's wrong?"

"Ah," Jane replied. "He's just gone off. Look, Emma, I can't speak for long. Mum's in hospital. He hit her hard in all the wrong places. Internal injuries. I can't believe it. She's in a real bad way. Dad found out . . . I can't say on the phone."

"Found out about you and Rick?"

"He guessed."

"Are you all right? Did he hit . . .?"

Jane interrupted, "Well, yes, he did. But I've known worse. I'm okay. Black and blue, maybe. Some Christmas this has turned out to be!"

"Are you sure you're all right?" Emma asked anxiously. "I could call in tonight, when we get back."

"No. It's Mum I'm really worried about. He really did . . . let fly this time. I just hope she'll pull through. But there's no point hiding Rick now. He's coming round tonight to try and sort it out. See what he can do, if anything. He's upset as well. Everything'll change now – it can't go on."

Emma's knuckles around the telephone were as white as her face. Last night's story ran rapidly through her head. "*The master flew into a rage . . . When he heard, vengeance came to Matty's mind. But it was a trap. Matty rode into a trap. It's still not over!*"

"No!" Emma burst out.

"What?" said the voice at the end of the line. Without giving Emma a chance to reply, she added, "Oh, Dad's just come back in. I've got to go."

Urgently, Emma replied, "Jane, you're in danger. You and Matty . . . I mean, Rick." It was no use continuing. Emma had heard the click of the receiver being put down. She did not know if Jane had heard her warning.

Emma ran through to her father's room. "Dad!" she cried. "We've got to go back. Jane and Rick are in real trouble."

Her dad held her shoulders and pushed her into a sitting position on the bed. "Calm down," he said. He knelt in front of her. "Tell me what's happened."

"Her dad found out about Rick. He's thumped her. I know he has. But tonight Rick's going to her house!"

"So?"

"It's Tess and Matty, Dad. I know it's silly but it's just like Tess and Matty. It's not over yet. Rick's in danger."

"That was just a story, Emma," her dad said softly. "Remember? A folk tale. I suspect there was some truth in it – there usually is – but I bet that each time the story's told it's embellished a bit more. Don't let it affect you like this."

"I'm sorry, Dad," she retorted, "But it's . . . uncanny, you must admit. Matty was a crook, but a good man. Rick's fine but he's got a record."

"Really? What for?"

"Shoplifting."

"I didn't know that," he replied. "Still, just a coincidence."

"Is it a coincidence that their fathers – Tess's and Jane's – both disapprove of their boyfriends? Neither's good enough for their daughters."

"Dads are like that," he said. "A little wary. A little jealous, even. Funny creatures, dads. Too protective, maybe."

"Funny way to be protective, Dad. They both beat up their daughters."

"Yes, well . . . Some fathers get overwrought."

Emma looked in her dad's face and thought she saw doubt in his eyes. He might not be saying so, but he was beginning to believe her. His concern was no longer restricted to the state of his own daughter. "You must see . . ." she began.

"Yes," he said, "I do see what you mean. I'm not that insensitive, Emma – there *are* parallels. I'd love to put the Woodwards to right as well, I promise you. I really would. For lots of reasons. But I see a practical problem. We're 120 miles away and between us and them is a fog that no one should have to drive through."

"But—"

"Look, we'll do a deal, Emma. I'll get Mike to give us the

first lunch. We'll eat up smartly then set out straight after. Hopefully, the fog will have cleared, but we'll go even if it hasn't. Okay? We can be back by five or six at the latest. We'll probably get to the Woodwards' place before Rick, even. Is that okay?"

Emma nodded. "Thanks, Dad. I feel daft about all this but . . . I'm sure I'm right. We really must do something."

"I think it's the best we can do," he replied. "But tell me," he added, "did you hear what Jane's mum thinks of all this?"

"Jane's mum?"

"Yes."

"Didn't I tell you?" Emma said. "She's in hospital."

"What?" Her dad looked quite shocked.

"Jane said he really let fly this time."

Under his breath, Emma's dad swore at Mr Woodward. "Is she going to be all right? Do you know?"

Emma shook her head. "I don't know. Jane was worried about her. Serious internal injuries, it seems."

Her dad stood up and went over to the window. Emma could not see his face but she guessed that he was mumbling another curse. "He really is a nasty piece of work, that chap," he said aloud. "It can't go on like this."

"That's what Jane said as well," Emma told him.

He turned resolutely. "You go and pack, Emma. So we

can leave straight after lunch. And," he added, "you'd better pray that this fog clears up."

It didn't. By the time they had finished their meal and collected their cases, the fog had hardly thinned. "Oh well," Emma's father commented. "We'll just have to be careful."

While they checked out, Mike reminded them to watch out for the highwayman on the Great North Road.

"In this?" Emma's dad exclaimed. "It'll be a struggle to see the road, never mind a ghost trotting along it."

Before setting off, he scraped the layer of ice from the car windows. The engine started reluctantly at the third attempt. He revved it up and turned on the headlights. White mist billowed in the beams but the road became visible for a few more precious metres. They drove out of the car park and immediately the hotel disappeared into the smokiness as if it had been spirited away. A few miles south of Wetherby they joined the southbound A1 – a string of bright orange street-lights which had been left on all day in an attempt to pierce the oppressive greyness.

At first he drove slowly, using the cats' eyes to guide him, always ready to brake if another car should loom out of the fog. He soon realized, though, that they could be the only people on the road. Everyone else was too sensible to attempt a Christmas Day outing. Gradually, he got used to the conditions and drove faster. Emma did not object. She was impatient to see Jane.

England sped past unseen. Its factories, countryside and towns had dissolved. What a Christmas Day! It seemed more like night – strangely silent and ferociously cold. Weeks before, the wind had made skeletons of the trees. Now, fog shrouded them. Most cars, white with frost, remained stubbornly and safely in drives. The treacherously icy pavements deterred all but the most adventurous walkers. The street-lamps just managed to dispel the murk around them, but the coloured lights decorating the roadside windows of the pubs and cafes were lost in the gloom.

"Dad?"

"Yes," he replied, not taking his eyes off the road.

"They're going to be all right, aren't they?"

"You mean, Jane and Rick?"

"Yes."

"Sure they are," he responded confidently, as if he really did know.

Emma looked at her dad suspiciously. He was tense but she had put it down to the strain of driving. Now, it dawned on her that he might have another secret.

He felt her gaze on him, probing. He turned his face towards her briefly. "All right?" he asked.

"I suppose so," she replied. "It's just that you sounded too convinced. As if you knew . . . Are you just trying to make me feel better?"

"Er . . . no. Not really. I just think they'll be okay. Actually," he said, "my brain was elsewhere. I was thinking about Sheila . . . I mean, Jane's poor mother. It sounds as if she's the one we should be most worried about."

"Dad?" Emma began to quiz him again. "Is there something else . . .?"

He interrupted her, "Just this damn fog." Then he added, "Oh, look. It's clearer here. I can put my foot down." Glancing back to Emma in the passenger's seat, he sighed. "It's no use," he admitted. "You can see straight through me. I'm sorry – I should've told you. I very nearly did when we first arrived at the hotel. It's one reason why we came – to give us some time to talk things through. But it's more difficult than I thought." The car lurched somewhat as he misjudged his speed around a left-hand bend. "Damn bends!" he muttered. Immediately, the road went into another bend. This time to the right. He braked hard. The wheels locked but the car did not slow. It just careered on. "Ice!" he screamed. "We're on black ice. Get your head down!"

The tyres screeched. Emma's dad cried in anger and dismay. He tugged desperately on the steering wheel but it had no effect. They were out of control. With a sickening thud, the side of the car crunched into a road-sign. The door caved in. The car spun round, rolled off the road and rammed an old oak tree. The engine cut out and the deathly silence returned.

The passenger door creaked open and fell off its hinges. Emma's arm dangled from the car and touched the ice-cold grass. She groaned. Her first instinct was to get out of the car as quickly as she could, but movement made her feel sick and every part of her body ached. She was confused, her head pounded and her eyes would not focus properly on anything.

She tilted onto her side so that both hands could touch the cold but solid ground. She used her arms to drag her body, slowly and painfully, out of the car. Her legs, as stiff as an old arthritic woman's, were the last to flop on to the ground. Emma cried out, possibly with pain, possibly for help. No one answered her. Crawling, she inched her way over the freezing earth until she thought that she was a safe distance away, then sat, exhausted.

She didn't care about the cold and damp. Slowly her vision cleared and she rubbed at her legs until she felt that they might move more freely and support her weight. "At

least," she surmised, "nothing's broken. I can move them."
As reason displaced shock, she realized that she had not
spared a thought for her dad. In following her instinct to
escape from the wreckage – in case it went up in flames – she
had not even glanced at him. Was he still in the car? Had he
been thrown clear? She hoped so. The car was a tangled
mess of metal. Groping at another tree, she yanked herself
upright. "If it hasn't caught fire by now," she said to herself,
"it's not going to."

She forced her legs to carry her forward. Staggering, she
made for the driver's side. As she bent down to look through
the hole that had once been a front window, she moaned
with the pain in her back. Her dad's head was lolling against
the side stanchion. On hearing her groan, his eyes opened.
With an unnatural gurgling in his voice, he said, "Emma.
Are you all right?"

"Yes. I'm okay."

"Thank God."

"But you . . ." She stopped herself. "I'd better try to get
you out of there."

"No," he snapped. "I think not. I don't think I'll be
leaving the car."

"You mean, you're trapped?"

"I think so. By my legs," he answered. "But I meant
something else." He turned his head away from her,

coughed, then turned back. "Listen," he said. "You don't have to worry about Rick. He's safe."

"What?"

"Rick and Jane. They're safe. You see, he's not the highwayman. I am."

"What?" Emma repeated, wondering if her dad was delirious.

"I'm the highwayman. Jane's mum and I . . . We . . ." As he tried to talk, Emma rested her hand gently on his shoulder. "We fell for each other as soon as we met, Emma. We've been seeing each other ever since. I didn't have time – or the guts – to tell you."

"You mean . . .?"

Clearly, it hurt him to move his head because he winced when he nodded. "We're lovers. That's the reason I wanted to get back. He must have found out. That's why he gave her such a beating. I think Jane guessed she was seeing someone but she didn't know it was me. Forgive me, Emma."

She wiped the sweat from his forehead and whispered, "There's nothing to forgive, Dad. I just wish . . . it could have been different."

"Take care, Emma."

"How do you mean?" she asked, aghast. "Dad! No!"

For the first and last time, she saw tears of regret in her father's eyes.

*   *   *

On Christmas Days, when fog descends on the A1, some drivers swear that they have been overtaken by a ghostly car. They see it first in their rear-view mirrors, as headlights emerging from the greyness. The car accelerates then speeds past, far too fast to take the bend ahead. They hear the squeal of the car's tyres, or maybe the anguished scream of its driver. It goes into a skid, thuds against a post and spins off the road. Then nothing. The drivers stop and breathe deeply to recover from the encounter. They get out and peer about fretfully, but there is no sign of wreckage. Just the outline of a twisted oak, beguiling fog and uncanny silence.

THE MEGOWL

Garry Kilworth

im Sully was dressed all in black, with a luminous green skeleton painted on his front. His face was a grinning skull behind which his worried eyes flicked to and fro as he hurried past the wild thickets that separated the houses. It was Hallowe'en and he had been out trick-or-treating with friends. His pockets were full of sweets and he had eaten more cakes and biscuits than was good for him.

Tim walked the lane that led to his house. It was only a short distance, not more than two hundred metres, but it was overshadowed by trees on both sides and very dark. Every so often he passed a house, set back from the lane in the trees. The lights from their rooms gave him a little comfort. Listening to his heartbeat, which seemed louder than the wind in the trees, he suddenly came in sight of his own house.

Tim felt a sense of relief. They had been scaring so many people that night that he had finally worked himself up to a pitch of excitement from which it was hard to descend. At thirteen he believed himself to be too grown up to get scared on Hallowe'en, but once his friends had left him at the turning to his own lane, taking their high chattering voices with them and leaving him with the silence and darkness of the October night, it had been a different story.

When he was twenty metres from the house, Tim suddenly stopped dead, the skin on the back of his neck prickling in fear. Something was moving in the unkempt hedgerows. Slowly he turned and stared at the spot from which the noise was coming. It was a kind of rustling, skittering sound and he told himself it must be a bird.

"It's probably only a thrush or something," he muttered.

To prove to himself that it was nothing out of the ordinary, he walked to the hedge and peered into the black foliage. With his heart pounding he reached out and gently parted the leaves. At that moment the moon found a gap in the clouds and illuminated a white object nestling in the fork in the hedgerow. The pale, ovoid shape seemed to invite Tim's touch as he reached out and, hesitating only for a moment, put his fingertips to the thing, which was an egg.

Tim's hand jerked back to his sides. The egg was warm. His common sense, as well as his instinct, told him this was very strange. It was October, the autumn leaves were falling and any eggs forgotten by birds in the spring should be stone cold by now. He could think of no birds that laid their eggs in October, just before the onset of winter, which would kill any newborn chicks. The egg of a wild bird, whatever it was, should not be warm. It should be dead, cold and rotten.

Was this someone's idea of a Hallowe'en joke? Perhaps it was a pullet's egg, or that of some other tame or domestic fowl. Maybe someone was hiding in the thicket, watching to see what Tim would do. Perhaps there would be a sudden burst of laughter in a moment and one of his schoolfriends would come crashing through the trees shouting, "Got you, Sully! Got you this time! Wait till I tell the others about this then!"

There was no laughter, however. The wind played chasing games with the darkness in the trees and a few more leaves fell. Overhead, a cloud passed in front of the moon, causing a brief blackness to envelope the scene, then the light returned.

The egg was still there, inviting touch. Tim impulsively reached out and grasped it in his hand. Without really knowing why, he ran towards the house, clasping it to him. It seemed to pulse in his fingers as he dashed through the open gateway and hammered on the door with the iron knocker. The sound echoed through the hallway, then he heard his mother's quick footsteps. The door opened.

Tim's mother, a tall woman with a narrow face, gasped and stepped back, her hand to her breast.

"Oh, Tim!" she wheezed. "I'd forgotten you were dressed like that!"

"Sorry, Mum," he said, slipping past her. "Didn't mean to frighten you. I'll go and change into my pyjamas"

Tim walked quickly to his bedroom, but stopped on the way to put the egg in a shoebox which he kept at the back of the airing cupboard, under a bundle of old newspapers. It was his hidey hole for treasures. Then he had a quick wash in the bathroom and took off the skeleton suit, replacing it with his pyjamas. He went to the living room to find his mother.

She was sitting by the gas fire, poring over some papers to do with her work. Tim's parents were divorced and his father lived in Lancaster with a new wife while his mother, Deborah, worked in a local estate agent's office. Though Tim occasionally saw his father during the holidays, the meetings were becoming fewer. Mr Sully seemed more interested in Susan, his new wife, and appeared to want a complete break from his former wife and son.

Tim was an only child so he got a bit lonely at times. His mother was often too absorbed in her work to have much time for him. Sometimes he wished she didn't work quite so hard.

"Sorry about that, Mum," Tim said again, as she looked up from her work.

"It's all right," she replied in her abstracted way. "I just wasn't expecting it. You off to bed now? Did you have a good time?"

"Yes. Dave was dressed in a sheet and Karen wore a witch's outfit."

"That's lovely, dear," she said vaguely.

Tim stared at his mother's wispy-haired head as she bent over her work and he sighed. She was a good mother in many ways but she lived in some hazy world which was hard to access.

"'Night, Mum," he said, kissing her cheek.

"'Night, Tim."

Afterwards, lying in bed, Tim considered the egg. He had never robbed birds' nests before tonight and wondered why he had done so now. The egg had seemed strangely attractive and he had felt a sudden urge to possess it. It had been a feeling impossible to ignore. Then there was its strange warmth, as if it were still alive. That was not possible of course. Either someone was playing a trick or some animal or bird had warmed the egg by accident. He would throw it away in the morning. He fell asleep, staring into the darkness of the room around him.

The following day, however, he had forgotten about the egg, which nestled in the shoebox in the warmth of the airing cupboard. Unknown to him inside the shell there were signs of faint activity – activity which increased as time went on.

Occasionally, Tim heard a rustling noise on the landing, but thought little of it. He thought nothing too, of the strange dreams he had from time to time. Dreams in which he was flying, or hunting in the dark. He certainly never thought of the egg. Indeed, he had forgotten its very existence.

Time passed swiftly and it was soon Christmas. Tim was very excited. His cousins would be coming for Christmas Day and he was looking forward to receiving his presents.

On Christmas morning Tim visited the shoebox again. Among the treasures inside it was a small present for his mother – a pair of sewing scissors. He had bought them in the summer, knowing the pair she already owned were getting rusty.

The scissors were there all right, but someone had been to his box already. The lid had been removed and was lying upside down next to it. Tim was just considering remonstrating with his mother for going through "his things" when he noticed the broken pieces of eggshell. He suddenly realised what had happened. Incredibly, the egg had hatched and the chick had pushed the lid off the shoe box to escape.

Tim stared into the depths of the cupboard, which housed the hot water tank and sheets, towels and pillow slips. He could see nothing – no signs of a bird of any kind. His mother would not be pleased to find droppings or feathers on her clean linen, that was certain. Finally he decided that the bird must have got out of the cupboard earlier, when his mother had opened the door. No doubt it was free, somewhere in the house. He would have to keep his eyes open for the creature.

When Tim's cousins and various relatives arrived the creature was soon forgotten in the excitement of exchanging presents. Tim got the pair of roller blades he'd wanted for ages, from his mother. They were the latest in roller skates and he and his cousins, who also had blades, went off to the local skateboard park to try them out.

Late in the evening the last guest left the house and Tim and his mother were alone again, clearing away and washing up together before going to bed.

"Have you enjoyed today?" asked his mother anxiously. "I'm sorry the turkey was overdone. I don't think your uncle Jim liked it very much."

"Never mind, Mum. Turkey's turkey – and the roast spuds were good."

Her eyes lit up a little at these words.

"Were they, dear?"

"Brill, Mum – take my word for it. And the roller blades are ace! Thanks a million."

She went to bed fairly happy after these words. Tim was always amazed at the power he had to make his mother cheerful or sad, and sometimes it frightened him. He did not want the responsibility for her happiness.

He put out the lights and went to his room at the back of the bungalow, where he stowed the roller blades in a cupboard before climbing wearily into his pyjamas. He tried to read a comic but his eyes kept closing, so he switched off the light and lay down to sleep.

It must have been about twenty minutes later that Tim woke to a strange sound. For a few moments he just stared into the darkness of the room, wondering what had roused him from his first sleep. Then he heard it again – a kind of rustling, scratching noise which seemed to be coming from the corner of the room. He peered into the dense shadow but his eyes could make out nothing except blackness. For a while nothing happened and Tim was dropping off to sleep again when there were further sounds.

He felt a trickle of fear go down his spine. What was it? Had a mouse got into his room? Maybe it had been attracted by Christmas cake crumbs or something. He and his cousins had been eating in the bedroom that day.

He wanted to get out of bed and look but a stronger feeling of fright would not let him. He was afraid of what he might find. Late at night there were things that worried him more than they might have done during the day. Things were different in the dark, in the silence of the small hours.

Suddenly, Tim reached for a book on his bedside table. He threw it into the corner and buried his head under the bedclothes. After a few moments he listened hard for the sounds to return and when they didn't decided it must have been a mouse after all – now frightened back into its hole. He would search the room tomorrow and block the creature's lair, wherever it was. The fear-sweat that had covered him earlier now began to leave and he was able to go back to sleep.

Later, however, he had the sensation of being disturbed by a faint rustling in the bedsprings, but it was not loud enough to wake him thoroughly and in the morning Tim wondered if he'd fallen asleep and dreamed it after hearing the scratching in the corner. It was always difficult to sort the real from the unreal after night fears.

An inspection of the bedroom after breakfast revealed no holes in the skirting-board. Remembering the broken egg-shell, Tim searched for fur and feathers too, but found nothing and convinced himself he'd been dreaming as a result of too much Christmas dinner.

"Had a bad dream last night," he told his mother.

"Did you, dear?" she replied vaguely. "How upsetting for you."

"Oh, it was no big deal," Tim added. "It wouldn't even seem scarey if I told you now."

"Fine," she replied. "Now I must get these papers finished before I go back to work tomorrow. Can you amuse yourself?"

"Sure," said Tim, leaving his hard-working mother to her problems.

Boxing Day was spent walking the downs and using the roller blades. It was one of those sharp, crisp winter days, where a low sunset throws out bright rays to make the frost glisten on the meadows and pick out crystallised spiders' webs in the hedgerows.

That evening, on returning to the house, Tim found his

mother still engrossed in her papers. She murmured something about "lunch" and Tim told her lunchtime had long
since gone and it was time for dinner.

"Oh dear," she said, pushing her glasses up her nose and
brushing away strands of hair from her eyes. "Never mind,
we'll have some turkey sandwiches in a moment. Will that
be all right?"

"Fine, Mum."

Tim went to his room to put away his roller blades. It was
gloomy in there, as the main bulb had blown and only his
small bedside table lamp cast a pale light over the corner. He
opened his wardrobe door and put the blades in the shoe
rack inside. As he did so he glanced up at the hanging coats.

Something white stared out from amongst their dark
folds.

Tim jumped backwards quickly, startled into uttering a
sound much like the yelp of an injured puppy. Fear gripped
him. It washed through his whole body like a wave of
freezing water. His breath came out in short, sharp pants.

He was immobilised, rigid with terror, as he stared at the
creature before him, perched on the coat rail.

It was a bird with the face of an old woman.

The creature's feathers were white. The complexion, with
its tiny, shrewish features, was a pasty grey. Prehensile claws
flexed on the coat rail. The creature spat at him viciously.

"Yetchhh!" it screeched.

Tim could do nothing but stare into the mean eyes of this nightmarish fiend. He want to scream for help, yell for his mother, but the eyes would not let him. They held him fast where he stood, their control over him complete. He could not even move his hands or feet.

"Eeerchh!" whined the owl, through the tiny, white, even teeth.

Tim's own teeth started chattering and he bit his tongue several times. Sensing his distress, the owl's human face produced a savage smile. Then some strange creaking words came from its mouth and Tim found to his horror that he understood them. Hypnotised, he closed the wardrobe door gently and went into the kitchen.

There he walked straight to the fridge and selected a piece of liver still swimming in a pool of blood. Taking some scissors from the cutlery drawer, he cut the raw liver into slivers and carried them back to his bedroom. He opened the wardrobe door again to find the terrible owl still there. Tim fed it the strips of raw liver, watching in disgust as it snatched them from his hand and swallowed them like worms.

When the creature was satisfied, it shuffled on its perch, said something in its dark, ugly tongue and closed its eyes. Tim shut the door on it and crept away, still chilled to the marrow by the encounter.

He went straight to the living room and stood in front of his mother. Her head was bent over her work but eventually she looked up at him.

"Goodness, Tim!" she cried. "Are you all right? You look so pale."

Tim wanted to tell her about the horrible thing in his wardrobe but his tongue would not let him. Instead he heard himself say, "I'm fine, Mum. Just a bit tired. I think I'll skip dinner."

"Skip dinner?" she said. "You must be ill. Go to bed. I'll bring you something."

He stumbled out of the living room, half in a dream, and went to his bedroom. There he changed into his pyjamas and got into bed. Later his mother brought him some turkey soup and he ate it. Then she pulled the curtains and left him alone.

That night he hardly slept at all.

Over the next few weeks Tim was haunted by the owl. It sat on the headboard of his bed at night and kept him awake by whispering foul things in his ear. It made demands on him, urging him to bring it pieces of raw meat. The creature began to grow at an alarming rate, until it was as large as a pillow, its creased, wizened face becoming more evil-looking with every passing night. It devoured everything that Tim could find in the house, until eventually he had to begin begging for meat from other places.

Tim himself began to change too, both in appearance and attitude. He was morose and glum, avoiding his friends until they began to shun him. His teachers became worried about him and sent notes home to his mother, telling her that Tim was falling asleep in class. These he threw away on the way home from school.

Eventually a teacher went to Tim's house and had a long talk with his mother, who confessed that she had had a crisis at work and had not noticed that her son was looking unwell.

"I'll take him to the doctor in the morning," she promised.

When she finally did take time to notice him, she saw how hunched he was, his head sunk between his shoulders and his arms dangling by his sides.

"Why are you standing like that?" she asked. "Oh, Tim, you do look a bit grey and worn. We'll have to see what the doctor says."

The doctor gave Tim a check-up but could find nothing wrong with him.

"It's probably one of these new viruses," he said. "They sap one's energy and leave one feeling listless and apathetic. Give him three of these tablets a day and see how we go on. If he needs rest, you'd better let him stay off school for a while. We'll have to play this one by ear. All right Tim?"

Tim gave the doctor a tight, wan smile, as weak as a winter sun. He had the words ready in his head to tell them all – the teachers, his mother, the doctor – but nothing would come out of his mouth. He longed to tell someone, to ask *anyone* what he could do about this dreadful creature which was destroying his life, but he couldn't. So he simply hunched deeper into himself and shuffled his feet, like an owl settling on a perch.

That night, when he took the owl some raw lights, the creature made Tim eat some too. Together, the human-faced creature and Tim tore at the soft giblets and intestines of animals which Tim had begged from the butcher, the juices dribbling down their chins and dripping on to the bedroom carpet. Tim had told the butcher that the raw innards were for his pet bird.

"What have you got? A kestrel hawk or something?"

Tim had nodded and muttered, "Or something . . ."

He wanted to be sick when the slimy giblets slid down his throat but the owl stared into his eyes and he found he could not bring up the disgusting raw meats and had to digest them.

"I hate you," he whispered to the owl and its old woman's face snarled and spat at him, telling him he was hers to use and he would have to eat far worse things before too long.

Anyone walking into Tim's room that night would have been shocked to the core at the scene. On one end of the bed sat the terrible owl, hunched into its feathers. On the other end of the bed sat the boy, hunched into his shoulders. Both creatures were uttering strange black words at each other, like two demons who despise each other yet are forced to live under the same roof. They hissed and spat and ground their teeth, the boy rippled his arms like wings and the owl shuffled her feet and sneered like a human. It was the most appalling and terrifying sight to witness.

Tim began to grow desperate. There was no one he could talk to about what was happening to him. No one would understand. He himself didn't understand. He began frequenting libraries and reading books on mythology, determined to discover what this creature was and where it had come from. Day after day he searched, but found nothing.

One day, Tim was lying on his bed trying to get some rest when his mother came into his room. She had his coat in her hands and she made straight for the wardrobe. Tim knew the owl was perched inside and he sat up expectantly as she opened the door.

She looked inside, gave a high-pitched scream, dropped the coat and ran from the room.

Tim followed her out a few moments later. At last, he thought, someone would do something to help him out of his nightmare. Instead, his mother was beside herself with anger. She was furious with Tim. He stood by helpless as she berated him.

"How could you?" she cried, shaking with annoyance.

"What?" pleaded Tim.

"You know very well – that horrible mask. You hung it in your wardrobe to frighten me. I don't know what's happened to you lately, Tim. You used to be such a nice boy. Now you're lazy and full of silly tricks like this. Mr James, the butcher, said you've been asking for meat from him for an eagle or something. I told him we hadn't got any kind of pet. What are you playing at?"

"I don't know," said Tim, close to tears.

"Well, I certainly don't know either," replied his mother. "Now if you'll go to your room, I'll try to get on with earning us some money, though I'm sure I don't feel like it after that ugly scare."

Tim lurched from the living-room, tears in his eyes. The owl seemed to have him trapped. He was its slave and he was becoming more owlish every day. He could no longer go to the butcher's so he would have to start trapping mice and rats. The owl's and, indeed, his own appetite was voracious. That evening he found some mouse traps in the garden shed and set them in likely places. Lately he had found his movements becoming quicker and his hearing and smell more acute. Perhaps he would soon be able to hunt without traps.

Just before the summer holidays, Tim finally discovered what he was up against. He found a book in the school library which somehow he'd missed before. It was entitled *Local Myths and Folk Lore*. Delving into it he came across a section entitled THE MEGOWL. It seemed that King Arthur's half-sister, the witch Morgan le Fay, had once passed through a remote corner of Essex. She had become displeased with one of the local witches, an old woman named Meg Hopkins, whom she had changed into an owl. The Megowl was a bird with a human face which laid one egg on Hallowe'en, then lived only until Christmas Day, dying the moment the new chick was born. It was, in fact, a rebirth – the old Megowl giving birth to herself through her own egg. Sometimes the egg lay dormant, waiting for centuries, for it had to be nurtured by a human child. Once the child was found, the Megowl gradually turned it into a creature like itself, so that it could more easily obtain food to feed her. And the worst thing of all, was that there was *no way of destroying it*.

Tim put the book back on its shelf and left the library, feeling bleak. He was indeed caught by a fiend, a demon who refused to let him go. Some of his former friends were off to the pitch to play football. They saw Tim staring after them and yelled cruelly, "There's the bird boy of Ashingdon! Why don't you flap your arms for us, Sully?" Tim bared his teeth like a savage animal and moved so swiftly towards the jeering youths that they ran off, leaving their football on the ground. Tim pierced it with his sharp fingernails, puncturing it. Then he made for the nearest ditch to hunt rats.

Several days later, Tim was called to the front of the class by the geography teacher.

"Tim, you don't seem to be paying attention. Are you sure you're well?"

"I'm never well," muttered Tim, burying his head in his shoulders and flexing his clawlike fingers.

"I see. Well, if you're ill you'd better go home, but we hardly see you lately, do we . . .?"

The teacher stopped in mid-sentence, for Tim had begun a peculiar movement, now familiar to him but so far not witnessed by anyone else. His throat was pulsing and his chest heaving violently. A kind of shudder was going through his whole body.

"Are you going to be sick?" cried the teacher, stepping back in alarm.

Suddenly the boy gave a kind of strangled cough and spat a large pellet at the teacher's feet. The wad which had come out of his mouth was made of fur and bones, packed together into a kind of bullet. It was in fact the regurgitated remains of a mouse that Tim had eaten earlier that morning. He had been unable to digest this pellet and, just like an owl, his body had rejected it.

The teacher took Tim's hand and led him immediately from the room. His mother was called on the telephone and came to collect him half an hour later. On the drive home, she questioned him.

"What have you been eating, Tim?" she asked, her eyes fixed on the road.

"Nothing," said Tim, sullenly.

"Tomorrow," said his mother, nodding, "tomorrow, we're going to the doctor's."

Hope surged through Tim's breast. He had been eating mice, voles and other small creatures for several weeks now. He knew exactly what he needed to do.

That night he climbed out of his bedroom window, under the sharp, piercing eyes of the Megowl. He had told her in her own tongue that he was going hunting. This was true enough. Tim intended to catch several small mammals.

He crawled into the nearest ditch, on all fours like a wild animal, and waited in the moonlight. When he heard a rustling in the hedgerow, his hand flashed out and snatched the small creature. It was a vole. The speed of his strike would have electrified any human witnessing this scene. Tim's movements were as fast as any wild predator's. He waited for a second creature to come along. Animals tend to use pathways they have made for themselves rather than cross open country, and Tim was waiting by one of these busy highways.

When he had several small, limp bodies, he went back to his room where the wizened-faced owl was licking her lips in anticipation. Tim fed her three of the mammals and ate two himself.

The following morning he was driven to the doctors. In the waiting room, he felt like regurgitating the pellet of bones and fur, but held it down until he was ushered into the surgery. As soon as he was standing in front of the doctor he let go and vomited the bolt of waste matter on to the desk. As expected, the doctor jumped backwards out of his chair.

"Good God!" he exclaimed. At once he examined the pellet then made a phone call. Tim was to be taken to the hospital for observation.

After a check-up, the boy was found to be in a weak condition, with worms and various other intestinal infections caught from the raw meat he had been eating. He was admitted to hospital.

His plan was working. At last he was out of the clutches of the Megowl.

Tim's mother was distraught. She was convinced that her son was going mad.

"Is it because his father and I got divorced?" she asked the doctors. "Is that why he's been eating these horrible things?"

The doctors were of the opinion that Tim was indeed deliberately trying to get attention.

"He probably feels rejected by his father," they told her. "And, as you say, you're very busy yourself, trying to earn a living. It's not an unusual situation. He needs to stay in our care for a while, until his physical health improves. Then we'll sort something out to help him mentally. He's not mad. He just needs some care and attention . . ."

That night Tim had the first real rest he had enjoyed in a long time. Snuggling down between starched white sheets, he felt cossetted by the hospital and its staff. The nurse called by every so often and there were three other patients in his room. It was like a fortress to him: a clean, stark fortress which would not permit entrance to a foul creature of the darkness. Tim was sealed inside a safe haven and he hoped that by the time he went home the Megowl would have either gone away or died of hunger. He thought of her vicious white face, ringed with feathers, and buried himself deeper under the bedclothes. She would be very angry. She would be spitting poison by now. He fell asleep.

Tim was kept in hospital for a fortnight, during which time he talked with the psychiatrist. He told the man that he had been having nightmares and after these dreams he ate things like mice and other small creatures. He still could not speak of the Megowl, for she had hypnotised him permanently, so that there was a blockage between his brain and his tongue. Every time he even attempted to tell someone about her, he experienced a kind of seizure during which his lips and tongue were locked and would not move. So he did the best he could, by laying the blame on nightmares.

The doctors were still convinced that the problem arose from his parents' divorce. His father was informed of his illness and came to visit him.

"I'm sorry to see you like this, Tim," he said. "Perhaps it's our fault – your mother's and mine – but sometimes people have to go their separate ways."

"I know all that," Tim said. "You told me before."

"Yes, well, it doesn't change with time. It's unfortunate you've taken it so hard – but I can't change, nor can your mother. We're as we are, and that's that. What I *can* do is see you a bit more. Would you like that?"

It was better than nothing and Tim nodded.

His father placed a hand on his shoulder. "We can start by you coming to stay with me for a while," he said. "Susan, my new wife, has agreed that we need to see more of you. Would you like to come to Lancaster for a holiday?"

"I'm not deserting Mum," said Tim fiercely.

"I don't expect you to. She agrees that a holiday will do you good and though we're divorced she still trusts me with your welfare. You are my son, after all. It'll just be for a holiday – nothing more. Then you can go back to your mother to live, but we'll still see a bit more of each other. What do you say?"

Tim nodded dumbly. He knew it would get him out of the house and away from that terrible creature.

That night, the night before he was to be collected by his father and driven to Lancaster, there was a scratching on the hospital window pane. As if in a dream, Tim got out of bed and slowly crossed the room. The other patients who shared the room with him were fast asleep. He lifted his hand and pulled back a corner of the curtain. There on the sill sat the foul creature which had caused him so much misery. Her grey-white features sneered at him, as if to say, "Did you think you could escape this easily?" She bared her white, even teeth and hissed some ugly words. Tim reached up, mesmerised, for the window catch. His fingers pulled at the handle but the window had not been opened for quite a time and it was stiff.

The Megowl screeched at him, jabbing the glass with her face, ordering him to pull harder so that she could get in. Her feathers were fluffed in fury and her owl-eyes blazed.

Just as Tim was about to give the handle a good hard wrench, a voice from behind him cried out,

"What do you think you're doing, young man?"

Tim whirled, to find the night sister watching him, amazed.

"I . . . I . . . er . . . nothing, Nurse."

"Get back into bed," she said, straightening the curtain, "and let's have no more nonsense."

Tim did as he was told.

Later that night there were more scratchings at the window, but Tim heard nothing. He had claimed that he could not sleep and the nurse had given him a strong sedative.

The next day his father took him to Lancaster.

Away from the Megowl, Tim gradually began to recover. He still looked fearfully at the windows at night and waited for the scratching sounds which meant that the creature had caught up with him again, but the sounds never came. His father's flat was in the middle of town. There was the comforting noise of traffic well into the night, running below the bedroom window. In the centre of a city, amongst modern houses, machines and industry, the idea of a supernatural creature, especially a being of the woods and fields, seemed faintly ridiculous.

Tim stayed with his father and Susan for several weeks. He found Susan pleasant and willing to please him, but he had little real interest in her. She was not his mother and she had no children of her own, so she treated him like an adult, which suited Tim fine.

The day Tim went back home, all his fears came rushing back. His mother was enormously pleased to see him, but he could hardly keep his attention on what she was saying.

"And how did you get on with . . . with Susan?"

"Oh, okay. She was all right . . ."

Tim then noticed his mother's worried look.

"She wasn't *you*, of course," he added quickly. "She was just someone else. You're my mum."

His mother looked relieved to be told this and Tim was pleased he had said it.

Once his mother had satisfied herself that he was glad to be home, Tim went on a search of the bungalow. It was past Hallowe'en – he had deliberately remained with his father until after that date – and he hoped the Megowl had gone. It should have set out to trap some other adolescent by now but Tim wanted to be sure. He looked in all the likely places – under the bed, in the wardrobe, behind the curtains – until it seemed certain that the creature had fled in search of a new slave.

With an enormous sense of relief, equal to that of his mother when she learned he was well again and had missed her, Tim went back to his normal life. November the fifth arrived, with all the excitement of Bonfire Night, and then the days fell away like leaves from the trees, until it was December.

December crawled by, for both Tim and his mother were looking forward to Christmas. Deborah had met a man she liked, a divorcee like herself with a daughter and son both younger than Tim. They were all coming to stay for Christmas and arrived on the evening of the 24th.

Tim liked Edward, his mother's new friend, and though the children were shy he wanted to make friends with them quickly. He knew it was important to his mother and he had never had the pleasure of young companions living in the same house. Everyone said "hello", smiled a lot, and went to bed early.

In the early morning Tim woke to hear noises in the kitchen. He crept downstairs to find Edward looking very sheepish.

"Sorry we woke you, Tim," said Edward, "I'm afraid I was a bit hungry and raided the fridge. I made myself an egg sandwich . . . I'm sure your mother won't mind."

He held it up for Tim to see.

Egg sandwich . . . Egg. Something suddenly clicked in Tim's mind.

Leaving a surprised Edward, Tim dashed out of the kitchen and went straight to the airing cupboard. Flinging the door open, he reached underneath the tank and found his old shoebox. Even as he pulled it out he could feel a movement coming from within.

The Megowl had laid its egg inside the box and left it to be incubated by the hot water tank.

Tim grabbed the box. Then he ran out of the house in his pyjamas and bare feet and along the lane to the main road. There were sounds coming from the box. He held the lid on tightly, his chest heaving with the exertion of the run in the cold morning air.

The thing inside the box began to struggle. Tim stopped, pulled out his pyjama cord from his trousers and tied the lid down firmly. He could not allow it to look at him. Once it looked into his eyes, he would be its slave again. Then, one hand holding up his pyjama trousers and the other clutching the box, he finally ran the last few yards to the road.

He waited.

A car went by.

The chick inside the box began gnawing at the cardboard.

Another car went by.

It was furious. It scratched and tore at the bottom of the box. In a few moments it would be free.

An open-backed Land Rover came into sight. Tim waited until it was level, then threw his burden with all his might. The shoe box and its contents landed in the back of the Land Rover and were taken away along the winding road, out of sight.

He was free at last!